My Love
Inside Me

My Love
Inside Me

ROSE MARIE
MACHARIO

Cover art: Randy Humphrey

Cover art in this book copyright © 2024 Randy Humphrey & Seventh Star Press, LLC.

Editor: Holly Phillippe

Published by Seventh Star Press, LLC.

ISBN Number: 9798344382265

Seventh Star Press

www.seventhstarpress.com

info@seventhstarpress.com

Publisher's Note:

My Love Inside Me is a work of fiction. All names, characters, and places are the product of the author's imagination, used in fictitious manner. Any resemblances to actual persons, places, locales, events, etc. are purely coincidental.

Printed in the United States of America

First Edition

ACKNOWLEDGEMENTS

I want to thank all of my Majick Of The Chosen Ones fans, who have crossed over into the dark side of my mind, and are reading this right now. Thank you...

I also want to thank my amazing editor Holly for editing this one, and for my awesome publisher Stephen to allow me to cross over from the fantasy realm into the world of horror. Thank you to you both...

DEDICATION

This book is for the fans of horror, and all things that go bump in the night…

CHAPTER 1: THE ACCIDENT

This is a story about how my life ended. I wouldn't say it all began on a dark and stormy night. Although, it was dark, and it was raining out…

My boyfriend had just picked me up from the club, and had started a fight over how much money I didn't make.

"I don't understand why it matters? Tonight was just a bad night. I'll go back tomorrow, and try again. We have plenty of money in savings right now, to cover our expenses," I stated.

"That's not the point, Rose. I'm having a hard time trying to justify you taking your clothes off in front of strange men for nothing," Johnny snapped back.

"I've been working at the club for years. There have always been ups and downs with the amount of money I make. Why is it such a big deal now?"

"Because I don't want you to work there anymore. If you're ever to be my wife."

"But…" I tried to stand up for myself, but he cut me off before I could.

"No. I'm finished talking to you about this. You're washed up as a stripper, Rose. You're getting too old, to compete with the twenty-something's anymore. I want you to retire from stripping," Johnny ordered.

"No, I won't. I'm not dropping it either."

We had continued to argue for the first few miles in his jeep, then I tried to take control of the situation. I thought perhaps if I gave him head it would calm him down like it usually did, but he waved my hand away. I persisted, reaching into his grey sweatpants for his cock. He usually went commando, which made it easier for me to manipulate an erection from him.

I unbuckled my seatbelt and leaned over his lap. I grabbed his hard member, and started sucking it gently. This always calmed Johnny down, but I could still sense his tension. I moved my hand up and down his hard shaft skillfully, using my tongue to trace circles around the perfect tip. His body relaxed even more, when I took all of him deep in my throat. We hit a bump and I gagged a little, but I regained my rhythm once again. Up, and down I bobbed my head onto his, using my tongue in unison with the circular motions of my hand. Using this technique always brought him to climax faster.

When Johnny's cock swelled even more in my mouth and his balls grew tight with my touch, I knew he was fixing to blow his nut. I forced my mouth over his cock now faster, gripping my hand tighter as it slid up and down the hard length of him. Johnny sucked in his breath, and then the salty bitterness of his load filled my mouth. It was right after that moment my world flashed before my eyes.

"Oh, shit!" Johnny yelled out, trying to swerve around a doe that had run out in front of us.

I was then thrown to the top of the jeep. It was a good thing the cover was on, or I may have been expelled from the car. I heard screaming, and then all went quiet.

When I finally came to, I was lying on the ceiling of the jeep. I wiped the warm trickle of something wet that had dripped onto my nose. I looked down at my fingers, it was blood. I must have hit my head on the dashboard, but I couldn't remember.

Johnny was hanging upside down, held tight by the seatbelt. I checked him for a pulse. He was still alive. I shook him gently, and then he opened his eyes.

"Johnny, are you all right? Can you hear me?" I asked.

"Yeah, I think so," he whispered.

"What happened? The last thing I recall is the fabulous blowjob you gave me, then I saw a deer."

"Don't try to talk. I'll try to get your seatbelt unfastened," I offered, then tried to unbuckle his seatbelt, but it wouldn't budge.

"It's stuck."

"Here, let me try," Johnny said. He fumbled with the button, but he couldn't even push it in. "You're going to have to go and get help."

"I'm not leaving you here. We're miles from the main road, and you know as well as I do, there's no cell phone reception here. I don't even know where my phone is?" I pleaded with him.

"You have to. I can't get out of this seatbelt, and the blood I think is now draining into my ears. Right now, you're my only chance, to survive."

"I don't want to leave you alone. I'll stay here until someone comes along. By dawn, this road will be busy, and someone will see us."

"Do you smell that?" he said, taking in another deep breath.

"Smell what?" I asked.

Just then smoke came up from the back of the jeep.

"Get out now. The gas tank must have gotten damaged in the roll, and if it did then the battery could spark. It won't be long before the jeep catches fire. Please, Rose, I need you to get out now!" Johnny shouted.

I began to cry. I didn't want to leave him. If I had to die in this jeep with him, I would.

"I'm not going. I'm staying here with you, no matter what!"

I shouted back.

"Why do you have to be so stubborn? Stop being a stupid bitch, and get the fuck out now!"

I jumped, when the flames erupted, from the front of the jeep. I was too scared to move. When Johnny touched my face and looked me in the eyes, I was able to calm down.

"Please, get out while you still can. I love you," he whispered.

"And I love you. But I still won't leave you," I cried out, before kissing him passionately in fear it would be our last. Off in the distance, I could hear sirens. I really felt that we were going to be saved. "I'm going to go get help!"

I looked at Johnny one last time. Sweat trickled down his brow.

"I'll be back with help, I promise. Everything's going to be alright." Those were my last words to my boyfriend, before I crawled out from the jeep.

The fire truck had pulled up, several feet away from the fire. I ran as fast as I could towards the fireman, who was climbing out of the truck.

"Please, you must save him!"

"Who, miss?"

"My boyfriend. I couldn't get his seatbelt unfastened. Please, you must help him. The jeep has caught on fire!" I shouted hysterically.

"Stay put miss, I'll do my best to save him," the fireman said, as he ran to the side of his truck.

The flames grew higher around the jeep, and I thought my heart was going to burst right out of my chest.

"You must hurry!" I shouted at the fireman.

My ears rang instantly, almost deafening me from the sound of the explosion. I was too afraid to look up. The firemen were putting out the flames, and all I could do was stand there and watch. I hoped that they were going to be able to save Johnny. I watched as they pried the driver's side door off. One of the firemen leaned inside the jeep for a few moments. When he came back out, he shook his head to the other fireman.

I wasn't paying attention to the fireman that approached me, until his hand gently touched my shoulder.

"I'm sorry, miss, but your boyfriend didn't make it."

Those words burned hotter than the flames that were put out. I couldn't even force a reply. I just stood there staring at the charred remains of my boyfriend's jeep.

"Is there anyone I can call for you, miss?" asked the fireman.

"No. I have no one else now," I whispered.

CHAPTER 2: THE HAUNTING

The next six months came and went. Johnny's family showed up, staying only long enough to bury him. They never liked me, and I shared the same affection for them…

When I first returned to our two-bedroom house, it felt so big. I had stayed with a friend after the accident and the funeral. But I was afraid to go back alone. I was so used to having Johnny there. He filled the place up with his personality and charm. Nicknacks of dragons and candles aligned the cherry oak finish wooden mantle over the fireplace. Gargoyles and more candles sat on floating black shelves, on the slate grey walls that he had painted himself. Now the house was only filled with his memory.

I had taken time off from work. Living off what little savings I had, and the small amount of money he'd left in his will. I was in no hurry to return to the job that Johnny hated.

I set my keys down on the granite counter, then walked into the living room. I stopped to kneel before the altar, on the far wall that was painted black. I lit a black candle and stared into the flame. I scried into the fire to meditate, focusing my mind's eyes on the solitary waving flame, as I drifted off into a memory...

"Johnny stop," I giggled from him tickling me.

"Stop what? I'm only playing with you," he teased.

"But I need to focus all my energies if this spell is going to work."

"I don't understand why you need to rely on magic every time you go to work."

"I told you it's because of this shitty economy. I need a little more of a guarantee I'll make money tonight," I clarified.

"I'm not saying you shouldn't try to have a better night, but you shouldn't do this. It will backfire on you one day. You can't rely on magic for personal gain. It doesn't work that way without repercussions," Johnny chided.

"Are you going to help me, or not?" I asked.

"Yes. I will help you," he said with a sigh.

"Thank you. Now let us focus together please."

"Fine."

We closed our eyes, and chanted in unison, "Money, come to me. Money that we need, money come to thee. So mote it be."

Johnny pricked my finger, and then his. We squeezed our blood into the mortar over a silver dollar that was placed inside. Then we each traced blood over our hearts, with the rune symbol for wealth. Our naked flesh was warmed by the fireplace, as we came together entwined in each other's arms. Our fingers locked, pulling each other into a passionate kiss. His tongue explored my mouth, as I explored his with mine. Hands fell to wanton flesh, caressing the hardened peaks of my nipples, as I reached down to grab an overflowing handful of cock. I stroked the hard length of him, while he reached between my legs to wet his fingers. I heard him draw a sharp breath, when I leaned down to take him into my mouth. I sucked him for only a few minutes to get it nice and wet for me. He pulled me off of him, as he turned me around pushing me down on all fours. My face hit the hard oak wood floor, as he pushed me down. He pulled my ass high in the air, before he buried his cock deep into my moist pussy. Holding onto my hips, he thrust himself deeper into my willing hole. I moaned as the sensations from his cock plunging in and out of me. His balls smacked back and forth behind me, as he fucked me harder. I could barely keep up with his thrusts, my knees were getting sore, and my hands were slipping on the floor. My head was yanked back, by the handful of hair he'd grabbed, as I was held tight in place.

Johnny leaned over and bit into my tender flesh. The warm liquid slowly dripped down my neck. He had a vampire fetish, and loved the taste of my blood. I let out a scream, but soon had a hand covering my mouth. His cock drove into my pussy even harder, my insides were being rubbed raw, and then my body began to shake. My loins ached, and my Kegel muscles contracted as I let go. Johnny followed my lead, and the warm gush of his cum filled me full. He slowed down his breath; it was hot on the back of my neck, as he leaned across my back. Cum dripped to the floor, as he pulled his semi-hard dick from me. We both rolled over on our backs in front of the fire.

"If that doesn't make you all kinds of money tonight, I don't know what will," he said breathing heavily.

I rubbed his sweaty chest with the back of my hand.

"I always do better going into work looking like I'd just been fucked," I agreed.

"You were just fucked. And it must have been good, by the amount of pussy juice I have all over my thighs," Johnny surmised.

"Yes, it was good," I said smiling. I hadn't been fucked like that in a few days. I needed that release.

"Well get up and go get your ass ready for work. It looks like it's going to rain tonight, so I'll drop you off. You can call me when you're ready to leave."

A noise from the other room snapped me out of my trance. I looked out the window from my place on the floor, but I didn't see anything. It was dark and could have been a tree branch falling, or an animal scurrying about outside. My attention returned to the black candle that had already melted halfway down. I had become aroused with the memory of our lovemaking, so I reached down to rub my aching pussy. Johnny was big on having sex following any ritual. He said it made our spells more powerful if we continued with the flow of energies, allowing for them to build stronger until it was released with our climax.

I put out the candle with the snuffer and retired to our bedroom. I took off the jeans and t-shirt I was wearing, tossing them into the hamper in the bathroom. I watched myself take off my bra in the mirror, then rubbed my breasts with both hands. My nipples went hard almost instantly, while I thought of Johnny. His touch always sent me into a state of arousal. I missed his hands on me.

I walked to the empty bed, pulling down the bedcovers. I crawled in between them and the cool sheet. Bumps on my arms erupted, and then I rubbed the chill away. After I rubbed my arms, I slowly let my hands slide onto my breasts again, then down my stomach. My clit swelled under the touch of my fingers. I rubbed my pussy before sliding a finger into the wetness. When I lay down on the bed to masturbate, I heard another noise. I wiped my fingers on the sheet and got up to check the window. It was dark, but I still didn't hear anything. Then the noise came again, but it was coming from the living room.

I walked into the room, and the cold set in almost instantly. I looked to the fireplace and the fire had gone out. It was too late to start the fire again, so I went back to bed.

When I returned to the bedroom, the bed was made. The blankets were neatly pressed and tucked under, complete with hospital corners. It was how Johnny always made their bed. I ran out of the room. I didn't know how to react exactly. I went before the altar and lit the black candle again.

"Johnny, if you're here please show me. Give me a sign," I whispered into the darkness.

I waited for a few minutes. It was as if he'd never truly left me, but I just thought it was because I wanted him there so badly. Nothing happened. I snuffed the candle out once more, then went back to the bedroom. I swallowed the bile that came up into my throat when I saw the bed. The covers had been neatly pulled down invitingly.

I walked past the bed, going into the bathroom and shut the door behind me. I put the toilet seat down to sit. Rocking back and forth, I managed to compose myself. It had to be Johnny.

I left the bathroom to go into the closet. I pulled a box covered in dust from the top shelf. I opened it and pulled the portrait of Johnny from the box. After placing the box back, I took the picture with me to the bed. My fingers shook as I traced along the image of my love. I closed my eyes and embraced the frame, wishing he would return to me. Johnny used to always tell me to be careful when wishing for something…

"Rose. What have I told you about wishing?"

"That I need to be careful," I replied.

"Why?" Johnny questioned.

"Because enough personal power can make the wishes come true," I stated studiously.

"Enough personal powers turn the wish into the will. The will is strong inside you. You can project your desires, and make things happen. You must be careful what it is exactly, that you wish for."

He always knew more than I did about myself somehow. I looked at his face in the picture one last time before drawing it to me and kissing it as I placed it on the nightstand.

Chills ran all over me as I crawled into the bed. My eyes fixed on the empty side. I pulled Johnny's favorite pillow to me, tucking it under my arm and between my knees. The silence was deafening. I lay there motionless, patiently waiting for the sandman to take me under his spell.

When sleep didn't come after hours of tossing and turning, I got up. I went to the kitchen and flicked the switch. The lights didn't come on. It was the middle of the night sometime, but I failed to look at the clock. I could see the numbers on the microwave. It was nearing three in the morning. I hadn't noticed how long I had lain there in bed, trying to go to sleep.

I opened the double refrigerator doors, to see what I was doing. I climbed on a chair, to check the bulb in the light on the ceiling. It was one of those bulbs that were supposed to last for months. How could it be blown out already? It seemed like I'd just replaced it. But I hadn't really been home in a while. I went to unscrew the bulb, and pulled back my hand quickly, placing my fingers in my mouth. I glanced to the wall I could barely see, but made out the switch was pointing down.

When I turned my head I was blinded, and then lost my balance. I got up from the floor, rubbing my ass. That smarted. The light shined brightly showing off the neglected kitchen. Dishes were piled in the sink, and set alongside it on the granite countertop. I shut the fridge door, and shook my head.

"I'll worry about cleaning the kitchen in the morning," I said to myself with a sigh.

I climbed back into the chair to put the glass dome back over the light. When I reached for the screws on the table, they rolled off onto the floor. I got back down to look for the screws and saw they'd rolled under the kitchen table.

I was on all fours under the table grabbing the screws,

when the lights went out.

"Owe, fuck!"

I rubbed my head and crawled out from under the table, only to stub my toe on the chair. I rubbed my hand over my face. Taking a deep breath and with screws in hand, I grabbed the dome, climbing up the chair once again. I fiddled with the light bulb thinking it was a connection that had gone bad. But I gave up, placing the dome back on. The light could wait until the morning.

I walked out of the kitchen, when the light clicked on again. Slowly I turned around to walk back into the kitchen. I looked at the switch on the wall, it was in the off position. Curiously I flipped it to the on position. Nothing happened. I wiggled it up and down. Still nothing. The light stayed on.

"What the fuck?" I whispered. I tried the light switch again. "Owe!" I put my finger in my mouth and jumped around. I shook my hand. "Fuck, that hurt." I gave up with the light, then walked away from the kitchen.

Once I was in the living room, I looked over and my shadow had disappeared from the wall. It was as though I was being watched, when I entered the bedroom chills crept over my naked skin. I let out a sigh, and saw it floating out in front of me.

It was at that moment, I knew that I wasn't alone.

CHAPTER 3: THE DISCONNECT

The small nuances and disturbances continued for weeks after the kitchen light incident. I grew tired of trying to fix the light switch, but they seemed to go on and off when I needed them to.

I finally had to return to work. I became stir-crazy sitting at home watching my things disappear and reappear in different locations in the house. I even went as far as super gluing the knickknacks on the mantle down, to prevent them from being moved into the other areas of the living room. But the glue didn't hold up for long. Chunks of the pieces were broken off and left on top of the mantle, and the knickknacks were still scattered about the living area once again.

Work had become my escape. I didn't take time out to socialize with the other girls, or gossip in the dressing room. I stayed out on the floor, hustling my ass off, to win over new customers, and trying to keep myself busy.

Performing on the fiberglass stage, under the skin – perfecting black lights, was my biggest way to keep my mind free from the goings-on at home, and also from memories of Johnny. Which seemed easy with the music pounding loudly in my ears from the four large speakers hanging in each upper corner of the room. Dancing also kept my mind distracted, as I swung around the stainless steel pole. Mindlessly, I hung upside down staring out onto the audience sitting at the round wooden tables and red upholstered metal chairs, as they threw money up onto the stage. Then I kicked my lean legs out at the same time, as I gripped the pole with my hands, flipping myself over. My black mary-jane style stilettos hit the stage floor, and I continued to dance as if no one was watching, while flinging my long black hair around. When the song was over, I heard the club's DJ call out my stage name thanking me for the beautiful show, then I exited to the back of the stage to the dressing room.

When I returned to the dressing room, one of my coworkers approached me.

"I'm so sorry for your loss. I've been meaning to tell you since the funeral, but I couldn't bring myself to say it. We all miss, Johnny. He was really cool, and a good bartender. He was the best we've ever had here actually. But I know he's got to be in Heaven right now watching over you."

"Thanks, Miller. But now is not the time to start preaching to me. If you'll excuse me, I have a customer waiting," I said walking passed her.

I couldn't stand that bitch, and I could care less how she felt about my loss, as she put it.

The night ended the same. The lights came on after all of the patrons had left, exposing the dirty, discolored carpet, and the once-matching burgundy carpet that lined the walls was now covered with years of dust. I counted my money, tipped the DJ, and readied myself to go home as usual. I couldn't wait to get out of there. Of course, on the way out the door, the manager stopped me.

"Gypsy, do have a minute?"

"Yeah, David. What's up?"

"I've noticed you've been here every night for the last several weeks. I know you're grieving in your own way, but you need to take a break. Take a few days off, and come back when you're ready."

"I really appreciate your concern, but I did take time off right after the accident. I've only been back a few weeks, and I can't take any more time off."

"Well, ok. But if you need anything, or decide to take time off later, just let me know."

"Thanks, but I need to get going now. Goodnight, David. I'll see you tomorrow." I couldn't get away faster than I had, and I left for home.

Once I had returned home, I wearily set my keys on the counter, walking through the house, without a care for its present condition, to my bedroom. I disrobed in the bathroom, placing my dirty clothes in the white wicker laundry basket. My nightly ritual included brushing my teeth, then washing away the war paint from my face, before crawling into bed. I kissed the picture of Johnny, then returned it to the nightstand, as I did every night. I worked myself to the point of exhaustion, just so I could sleep. But my sleep was frequently disturbed, by my nightmares of the accident. I couldn't let it go.

Day after day, night after night I worked nonstop for the next several weeks. I followed the same monotonous routine of work, then attempted to sleep. I could barely eat, and my clothes were hanging onto my narrow hips. A few of my coworkers asked from time to time if I wanted to get together for breakfast after work, at one of the local dives on the corner. But I couldn't bring myself to go, gave the excuse of being tired, and would go back home to finish my daily routine. Then it appeared as if my life seemed to stop. My coworkers stopped asking me to join them at breakfast and finally stopped talking to me altogether, all but my best friend Jem. She had always been there for me after the accident, and she never gave up, even when I pushed her away.

"How are you holding up, chic?" Jem asked.

"I'm fine," I said, trying to force a smile.

"Honestly, hun, we're all worried about you. I've been really worried about you too. Have you been eating, or sleeping?"

"Not much of either, I'm afraid."

"Is there anything I could do to help?" Jem said, petting my hair affectionately.

"No. I'm fine. I'm just going home. I'll call you tomorrow."

I left work the same as always.

My evenings at home consisted of staring at the television. Cable networks were my only friends. I would almost go into a vegetative state at times while watching our favorite shows, then cry after I had watched them.

I was crying all the time. Aches and pains followed the tears, and I no longer had interest in anything. No longer did I sit and stare at the television. No longer did I want to try and eat anything. No longer was I able to even sleep at all. I worked as much as possible, and I even pulled two shifts within the day.

The day shift girls only met me in passing, so I was not a matter of their concern. I came and went as I pleased, and not even my closest friend I'd ever had over these past several years, could get through to me.

"Gypsy. You're working yourself into an early grave. Is that what you want?" Jem said one night after work.

"I don't know what you want from me? Why won't you

leave me be?"

"Because I fucking care about you, that's why. You've not slept, you're working constantly, and your ribs are showing." Jem walked over to me and ran her fingers along my waistline. "What happened to my best friend with the hot, voluptuous figure, and the great sense of humor?"

"I don't know, Jem. She's gone, I suppose."

"She's not gone. She's in there somewhere, and I aim to get her back."

She tried to kiss me, but I had avoided her by gathering clothes from my locker and shoving them into my duffle bag.

"Don't bother. She's not coming back. Her life ended when Johnny died. All right, are you happy now?" I said, as I was trying to walk away from her, but she grabbed my arm.

"You have to let him go, Rose, he's gone. Let him die, will you?"

"He's not gone. He's still with me," I said, before walking towards the door.

"Magus has asked about you. You've not been to any of the coven meetings, and he's worried about you. What do you want me to tell him?"

I stopped where I stood, without looking in her direction.

"Tell him. Tell him if he really wants to talk, he knows where I live. I won't be coming to any more meetings. I planned on leaving the coven anyway."

"Why? Why would you leave us? This is the time when you need to lean on the coven the most. We can help you through this," Jem called back to me.

I finally turned around to face Jem. Her striking almond-shaped green eyes made me weak when I looked into them. She made an attempt to wipe my tears, but I brushed her hand away.

"No, they can't. And neither can you. No one can," I said, then walked away.

CHAPTER 4: THE POSSESSION

The drive home had become nearly dangerous. I kept falling asleep at the wheel. No matter how loud I turned the radio on or had all the windows in the car rolled down, I was still drowsy. Only when the lights from the passing cars blinding me, would startle me awake when I drifted off to sleep. When I finally arrived home I went straight to my bedroom, took off all my clothes, and crawled in bed. I had no more energy, not even to wash the makeup from my face. I was fast asleep before I knew it.

While I was sleeping, I woke up to an erotic dream. But it felt real. Hands were on me, slowly, softly, touching me with the uttermost intimate caresses. My legs were spread apart, and delicate kisses were placed along the inside of my thighs. Then my labia parted, with what seemed to feel like a wet tongue, probing the inner, moist folds, of my pussy. I tried to arch my hips into whoever tasted me fully, but I was pinned to the bed. I started to panic, I couldn't move at all. I opened my eyes and saw I was really being pressed into the bed. It wasn't a dream at all!

My arms were being pinned over my head with what seemed to be one hand, while the other hand was groping my breasts. Nipples were being pulled on, and my breasts were now being squeezed hard. I tried to scream, but something was shoved into my mouth.

Scratches appeared on my thighs as they were once again spread apart. An invisible mouth covered my entire pussy, while being devoured like never before. I couldn't stop it, but at the same time, I didn't want it to. I gave up the struggle, allowing my body to betray me. The hands explored my entire body, leaving nothing untouched. Fingers penetrated deep inside me, tongues licked me, teeth bit me, and a mouth covered mine, kissing me until I couldn't breathe. If this was a dream, I didn't want to wake up.

A body lay over mine, pressing me into the bed. Then a large dick pressing up against my thigh threatened to enter me. Do I dare let this strange entity take all of me? I didn't care. My pussy was throbbing with desire, and dripping with need to be filled completely with that invisible hard phallus.

As if the entity read my mind, it entered me without mercy. I screamed from the initial pain of feeling my pussy being penetrated. I spread my legs wider to accept it going in deeper. It made its first hard thrust, and it went all the way up into my core. The second thrust took me by surprise when my head was pushed into the wall. This being was toying with me. Just the way Johnny toyed with me.

Every deep push of this cock inside me sent a shudder through my entire body. The rhythm it created was no longer slow, but increasingly getting harder, and faster. I wrapped my legs around the force that was over me, and in me, counter thrusting, receiving it fully now. As the thrusts became more rhythmic, hands, mouth, and teeth, were all over my body once again. All of my senses were challenged right now. I didn't know where to put my hands, which were now free from its grasp. I allowed my body to go limp, while this thing took me over, and over again.

When I found myself losing control, I couldn't imagine

what it would feel like for this creature to cum inside me. Would it? Is it capable? The next moment, my vagina squirted uncontrollably, soaking my sheets.

Before I knew it, I was flipped over onto my stomach. My hips were pulled until my ass was straight up in the air. It then entered me from behind, filling my sore swollen pussy full again, with its large hard cock. I let out a scream when it hit bottom. The being fucked me hard, pulling my hips into it with such a force, I thought I would pass out. I came again, creaming the insides of my thighs.

It ravaged my body. It shoved its cock in every hole I had, shoving it into my mouth, shoving it into my ass, and then it pushed its cock back into my pussy, filling me full. It dripped out of me slowly, as I lay there in a puddle of cum on the bed. I couldn't move.

I drifted off to sleep. I was no longer being sexually assaulted, by the invisible being, that had made me have orgasms that I'd never experienced before. Was I dreaming? I'll never know. But what I do know is, that if it was to happen again. I wouldn't stop it.

CHAPTER 5 THE AWAKENING

The next morning, I had awakened feeling like a completely new person, with more energy, and happier for the first time in months. My newfound energy, allowed me to accomplish, the much-needed tasks I had to do. I had become so behind in the daily chores, due to my depression. Now it was time to clean my house and catch up on some dirty laundry.

After I'd finished with my chores, I began getting ready for work. I dropped one of my heels on the floor, I reached for it, but before I had bent over, it went under the bed. I went down on my hands and knees to reach under the bed for the shoe, which I must have kicked it under there accidentally. I blindly reached for it in the narrow space, and could barely touch the heel of the shoe, so I lay on the floor shoulder deep under the bed. I finally managed to grab the shoe and got up from the floor, to finish packing my bag for work.

At the club, I danced like never before. I accomplished pole tricks no one had ever seen. It was almost like I was a superhero in stilettos. Swinging myself around the pole incredibly fast, hanging upside down with one arm, and with my legs in a split no less. I rocked the stage, and set the record for the most couch dances done in one night. Every guy in that place wanted me. I could feel it, and sensed their desire for me.

It was as if I was experiencing an ethereal high of some kind. Everyone noticed the sudden change in me. The customers, my manager, and especially my best friend noticed I was not the same.

At the end of the night, Jem approached me.

"Look at you. What is the big change? Don't get me wrong I'm happy for whatever has happened to make you better again. I just want to know your secret," she asked.

"There's no big secret. I think it was the fact I'd finally caught up on my sleep," I replied matter-of-factly.

"You definitely look well rested. In fact, you look almost radiant." Jem slid her hand down the side of my face, then brushed my hair back away, and smiled. "Now there's my girl, I knew you were in there somewhere. I've missed you."

We kissed briefly on the lips. Then we paused to look at each other for a minute. I leaned in to kiss her again softly. When she didn't move, or kiss me back, I was embarrassed.

"I'm so sorry, Jem. I shouldn't have done that."

"Don't be sorry. I've been waiting a long time for you to kiss me," she said. Jem put an arm around me and pulled me closer to her.

We were already half naked from changing out of our dance clothes since it was closing time. Jem kissed me fully, our lips parted to allow tongues to slip into each other's mouths. Slowly, entwining tongues danced, as we kissed passionately. I grabbed the sides of her head, kissing her deeper, she returned fevered kisses, then her hands began to explore my body. She glided her hands down my back, then grabbed my ass, pulling me to her even closer. I then let my hands slide to her nice round ass, as we began to rub our soft bodies into each other. Jem's hands came around my hips, caressing my flesh up and down, until she reached my full breasts. She cupped them in her hands while she kissed me, then began to play with my hard nipples. I pulled her away from my mouth by grabbing a handful of her long red hair, as I licked down the side of her neck. I took her by surprise when I nibbled the soft curve of her neck. I resisted breaking skin, but I craved the taste of her blood in my mouth. When I bit down hard, I shocked even myself. She was so turned on by it, that she even didn't notice the tiny bead of blood drip down her back. I returned my mouth to hers, so she could enjoy the flavors in my mouth.

Jem pushed me down in a chair and then sat in my lap. I removed her bra, quickly latching my hungry mouth over one of her tiny pink nipples. Then she removed mine to free my larger breasts, exposing my rosy-hued nipples. She fondled them in between petite fingers, as we continued kissing each other. I rubbed my hands over her thighs that rested on top of mine. She was wearing a tiny see-through thong, which made it easy to slide over. Her pussy was very wet when I parted her lips with my fingers. She rocked herself onto my hand as I entered her. We kept kissing and touching each other, as she fucked my fingers.

When she stood up, I sat her in the chair, getting down on my knees in front of her. I spread her legs apart, pulling her panties to the side once again. I nuzzled the red racing strip on her pussy, before plunging my tongue deep inside her. She grabbed hold of my hair, sliding her ass down in the seat, so I could bury my face further into her wet muff. My fingers slid into her once again, while I sucked on her hard pink button. She came hard, soaking my hand, as I finger fucked the shit out of her, while teasing her clit with the tip of my tongue.

After she came again, I came back up placing my knee into her pussy on the chair, then kissed her again so she could enjoy her sweetness. I rubbed my knee into her crotch, making her cum again. She pushed me off of her, turning me around and bent me over the chair. She stuck her tongue between the cheeks of my ass, working her way down until she dove her face tongue deep into my wet throbbing pussy. I held onto the back of the chair while she ate me. Then she had me prop my right leg on the chair, so she could come around from the side. Jem got her fingers wet, as she worked my hot snatch from the inside. I lost control, bucking my hips into her hand and face. I grabbed a handful of her long red hair to hang onto, as she continued to finger fuck me. I came so hard, that I was embarrassed, as I squirted all over her face. I leaned down to help her lick it off, and our tongues entwined again. We were both on the floor now, the sixty-nine position, as we savored each other, moaning softly at the pleasure we were giving to each other.

I'd never been with a woman like this before, but it was as if I'd fucked women my entire life.

I made her cum again first, my face was glazed like a donut. And then I came right after her, washing her face with my juices again. We sat up and kissed a few more minutes before we stopped to rest. Her long red hair draped over the pale white skin of her petite shoulder. She was so beautiful, with curves in all the right places, and she was all mine.

"I want to thank you for such a lovely morning, but I have to go. I must go home, and feed my cat," Jen almost purred out the words.

"It was nice wasn't it? I hope I'll see you again soon?" I awkwardly said, before Jem kissed me softly again.

"Yes. I'll come by next week, if you'll take a day off," she said, while teasing my nipple with her fingers.

"I will make it a point to take a day off, for you," I whispered into her ear, before I began to nibble on her earlobe.

She pushed me away and giggled.

"I'll see you next week."

I kissed her once more, before I helped her put her clothes

back on. As I was putting on my clothes, I watched her walk away. I couldn't wait to see her again.

CHAPTER 6: THE OBSESSION

I arrived home later that morning. Too wound up from making love to Jem earlier, that I wasn't in any danger of falling asleep at the wheel.

My energy levels were still going strong. I removed my make-up and washed my face. I took off my clothes, they still smelled of her, and then I threw them in the dirty clothes hamper.

When I crawled under the covers, I picked up the picture beside the bed.

"I think I can finally move on with my life now," I said to the photo. I kissed the image of Johnny, then set it back down on the table. My toes reached the bottom of the bed as I slipped myself into a more comfortable position. Goosebumps crept all over me, and I cuddled myself deeper under the blankets. Just as I was getting warmed up from my own body heat, and was finally comfortable, I heard a voice.

"Rose."

It was faint, and I thought it came from outside. Sitting upright in bed, I listened for a few moments, and I could no longer hear it. I shrugged it off as perhaps the neighbors being really loud. I settled back down in the bed and slowly faded into sleep.

I opened my eyes. The sun was brightly invading my windows. I could've sworn I had the curtains drawn closed. I squinted my eyes for a minute or two to acclimate them to the day. I rolled over to look at the alarm clock. It was seven in the morning. I only had a two-hour nap. How nice. Sleep was not a luxury that I could afford to miss. So I rolled back over, to avoid the sunlight. I knew if I got up to shut the curtains, I would be wide awake, and functioning. That wasn't happening, my ass was staying in bed. Fuck the curtains. I closed my eyes again trying to lull myself to unconsciousness.

"Rose."

My eyes opened immediately. I could have sworn I heard someone say my name.

"Rose," the voice called again.

I sat straight up in the bed. I gripped my pillow to my chest. My heart fluttered out of beat.

I got up to look out the door peephole. No one was there. I checked the backdoor in the kitchen. No one was there. Maybe I was dreaming?

"Rose."

What was going on? I could hear a voice, but I couldn't see anyone outside.

"Rose!" The voice was loud this time.

It was as if it was in my head. Was it? I went to the altar to light the black candle. It could've been Johnny trying to make contact. I closed my eyes to focus my energy.

"Rose, can you hear me?"

"Yes, I can. Johnny, is that you?"

"Yes."

"Oh, Johnny. I've missed you so much. How is it you're here?"

"I never left you. I promised you, I would never leave you."

I opened my eyes and looked around the room.

"Where are you?"

"Go look in the mirror, Rose."

"The mirror? Why?"

"Rose, trust me. Now go to the fucking mirror."

I stood up, then walked into the bathroom. I looked in the mirror, seeing only my reflection.

"Now what?"

"Look deeper, Rose."

I didn't understand, but I did as I was told. I stared into the looking glass, but nothing happened. My eyes became dry, and I blinked. When I opened them, I saw Johnny staring back at me.

"Hello, Rose. Nice to see you."

I raised my hand up to touch the image.

"How?"

"I'm inside you. We are one now," Johnny whispered.

"What? What do you mean? How is this possible?" I said slowly, backing away from the mirror. I wiped the tears from my face. I couldn't breathe. My chest tightened, and I thought I was going to pass out. I sat down on the toilet seat to catch my breath. I could still see Johnny's reflection in the mirror.

"Take a deep breath and calm down. I'm not here to hurt you. I'm here to be with you. Just as I said I would. I love you. You know that, Rose. Don't you?"

"I need a few minutes here. Ok? I'm trying to get my head around all this right now. I watched you die. I spent months trying to get over you. I've moved on with my life."

"Yes. I know you have. She's a pretty little piece of ass too. I'm proud of you, Rose. You performed an excellent show last night," he smirked.

I jumped up and ran to the mirror.

"How did you know about that?"

"I was here the whole time. I saw everything."

"How? When?" I said, pacing the bathroom floor. "How in the fuck, did this happen?" I questioned, freaking out.

"Calm the fuck down. Stop being so melodramatic. You're

a witch. Don't act like you've never heard of spirit possession."

"Yes, I get that. But, why me?"

"So we can be together forever, Rose."

I turned around, left the bathroom, and then I shut the door. I went to the bedroom and climbed back in my bed.

"Go ahead, Rose. Hide under the blankets, like the scared little girl that you are. You can't run away. I will always be here for you," he said, which almost sounded threatening.

"But, you're dead," I whispered.

"I'm gone only in body. My spirit still lives, and now I live in you."

"I don't want you to live in me. I love you, and you will always be in my heart, but I don't want you to be literally!"

The pillow hit the far wall of the bedroom before I stormed back out. I went into the kitchen. I knew I had a bottle of Jack somewhere in here. It was for emergencies, and this was an emergency.

"Ah, ha. Here it is." I opened it and drank straight from the bottle. When I came up for air, my throat burned. I coughed and gagged on the fiery liquid.

"Getting drunk isn't going to make me go away, you know," Johnny stated.

"Maybe not, but I can sure as hell fucking try," I said, taking another swig. "It will at least dull my senses enough that I can't hear you," I added.

"Put the bottle down, Rose," he told me.

"No, I won't, and you can't make me."

Suddenly my arm went numb, and the bottle fell to the floor.

"What the fuck?"

"I can control you, Rose. I can control your mind, and your body," he informed me.

"You can't do that. Why would you do that?" I stammered.

"I told you. I want us to be together forever. We can make

this work. I promise if you do as I ask, I won't have to force you to do things."

"What is it that you want from me? What do you need? Is there unfinished business you have? I'll help you move on, if that's what you want," I asked.

"I don't have any unfinished business. Except for you, Rose," Johnny confessed.

CHAPTER 7 THE IMPRISONMENT

Weeks went by. Johnny kept me hostage in my own body. He wouldn't allow me to go to work, and I remained at home now, at all times. I tried to reason with him, but that didn't work either.

"Johnny, please. I've not been to work, you're not letting me eat, and I couldn't even sleep if wanted to. You're in my head talking constantly, and I need to rest," I pleaded.

"We have everything at our disposal here. There's no need to leave," he said, as if it weren't that big a deal.

"What about food? What about paying my bills? I have to go out sometime."

"With me inside you, there's no need to eat. I supply more than enough energy for the both of us. You can pay the bills online. Any more excuses?"

"They're legitimate reasons, not excuses. I can't live like this," I cried. I wanted my life back.

Johnny had also begun using me as a catalyst, for some spells he was working on. He kept my senses dulled during these times, not allowing me to see, or hear what he was up to. The only thing he told me was, that the spell would keep us together forever. I had always hated it when he shut me out.

"Johnny, please don't block my senses. It's so dark in here

when you do that. I'm trapped in my own mind with nothing else to do."

"I promise I won't take long, Rose. Just relax your mind. Take this time to rest, I'll take care of everything."

That's exactly what I was afraid of. A few moments later I was cut off from my body, like a switch had been turned off. It was dark now, only silence was heard within my mind, until it began to play memories. Like movies on a reel in an old theatre, the lights slowly came on, and began to play from the collections of the past...

I was running late for work as usual, when I arrived I was getting rushed to change, and get out on the floor. I heard in the back that David had hired a new bartender. That didn't mean anything to me, I didn't care. The old bartender was a dirtbag, and he harassed the girls for sex all the time. I was glad when he got fired. He had only tried to hit on me once, but I put him in his place right away. But after that, he was a total dick to me and all the other girls who had refused to sleep with him.

I walked onto the floor, and David motioned me over to meet the new bartender.

"Gypsy, I want you to meet, Johnny. He'll be the new bar back. I'll leave you to show him around, tell him a little bit about the rules around here. I'm late for a meeting, but I'll be back later on. Johnny, this girl has been with us for eight years. She's been here longer than anyone else, and she'll be the best person to show you around and introduce you to the other girls. I'll see you guys later," David said.

I watched David leave and turned my attention to the new guy.

"So, you're the new bartender? My name is Gypsy, and I'll be your tour guide this evening. Just kick back and enjoy the ride. Keep your hands and feet to yourself at all times. And I mean it. Stay away from the girls. They're off-limits. Our last bartender got himself fired for sexual harassment. Don't let it happen to you," I informed him.

"Did he sexually harass you, Gypsy?" Johnny questioned.

"He tried. It didn't get him anywhere," I added.

"I got it. I have to keep my big dick, in my pants. Not a problem."

"Aren't we just being a little arrogant?"

"No. I'm just being honest, Rose."

"Wait," I pushed him to a stop, "how do you know my name? My real name."

"Oh, I think David mentioned it. That is your name, isn't it? I prefer to call you by your real name. If that's not a problem?" He asked.

It wasn't like her boss to give up the girls' real names. There was something about him. I just couldn't put my finger on it.

"Yes. That's fine. Just don't mention it to anyone else. I like to keep my privacy around here. Especially from customers, you never know who might be a stalker," I warned him.

"That's right, you never know, Rose."

The way Johnny said my name melted off his tongue like hot butter. Through his dark sarcasm, I was still immediately attracted to him. He wasn't the kind of guy I usually went for. He was very tall, with broad shoulders, blonde hair, and green eyes. I normally went out with short, dark-haired guys with bad attitudes, like the last bartender. Even though I'll never admit it, I fucked him one night after work on top of the bar. He wasn't worth the time I gave him, but I was drunk and desperate. Even my best friend, Jem didn't know about him. It happened before I met her, so I never bothered to mention it. I could say I had a soft spot for the bad boys. This new guy Johnny, I could easily see myself hooking up with him.

Not even two weeks after that, we were constantly together, and always on the phone talking to each other. It was like a dream. He seemed perfect for me, in every way. Everyone at work adored him, but we kept our relationship a secret until we decided to move in together.

Johnny had a little house, out in the sticks. I mean, this house was out in bum-fucked Egypt, for sure. It was a long commute back and forth to the club, but he loved the peace, and quiet. There was only one other house about a quarter of a mile up the road. Often times the neighbors were so loud, you could hear them from the house. It didn't take long for me to move in. We hooked a trailer to his jeep, and without having too many personal possessions, everything was taken in one load.

Life with Johnny was great. We got along famously, and the sex we had was fabulous. Everything was perfect, for the first six months that we were together…

The light returned, and I could now see through my own eyes again. I could feel my hands and could move them. I was finally in control over my own body again.

"Rose, I'm back, Rose. You can return to your normal functions. I'm finished for the day."

"Are you still going to keep me in the dark, about what you're doing?"

"You'll find out in due time. For now, let us just enjoy each other, shall we?" He stated.

"How am I supposed to enjoy you being in control of me? When are you going to finish your business with me?" I asked.

"Rose, do we have to go over this again? I'm not going anywhere. You're stuck with me. Just as we promised each other when you moved in with me here. Now, what would you like to talk about?"

"I don't want to talk anymore. I'm done talking. I'm hungry, my body needs to be fed."

"Well, I'm not going to stop you. Go into the kitchen and make something to eat. I'll even turn on the lights for you," he offered.

"I also need sleep. It's two in the morning. My body needs to rest. Will you please let me go to sleep?" I pleaded with him.

"Eat first, Rose, and then I'll let you sleep. I promise. I keep forgetting sometimes, because I don't have to do either of those things. When I take over your body I don't crave food, or sleep as you do. I'm sorry, Rose. I'll try to take better care of you," he promised.

I ignored his apology and walked into the kitchen. I had nothing in my cabinets. I haven't been allowed to go anywhere since he began talking to me. Once he took control, I had no other choice, but to listen. The refrigerator was bare also, except for something covered in mold that I can't remember what it used to be.

"I have no food. I'm going to the store tomorrow whether you like it or not. Now, if you'll be quiet, I'm going to bed," I told him.

"Goodnight, Rose," Johnny whispered.

I went to the bedroom and crawled in bed. I was so tired, I couldn't keep my eyes open a moment longer. I lay there motionless trying to let my body drift off to sleep. My mind, however, would not rest.

CHAPTER 8 THE TORTURE

Johnny remained silent, during the night. However my mind still betrayed me, and my thoughts kept replaying the past. My life had become a broken record, skipping through all the bad memories. I figured somehow Johnny had a part to play, with the selected feature presentations.

I got up from the bed and headed for the bathroom. I sat down to pee and realized how badly I needed a shower. A hot shower did sound like a great idea. I stripped out of my pj's and turned the water on to heat up. While I waited I brushed my teeth, looking at my reflection in the mirror. I turned sideways, then turned to the other side. My ribs were showing, and my hips stuck out. My skin was ghostly white, and my black hair was dull.

I stepped into the shower letting the warmth embrace my body. It was comforting. I took my time letting the water run down over my head, soaking my waist-length hair, then I shampooed and conditioned it.

I scrubbed the weeks of grime from my body, enjoying the roughness of my loofa. When I picked up my razor, I stared at it longingly. I erased the idea from my thoughts and proceeded to shave, but the vision of me watching the blood wash away down the drain still enticed me.

I stepped out of the shower and dried the wetness dripping from my body with the towel. I flipped my hair over and wrapped the towel around my head. I wiped the mirror and saw Johnny's reflection.

"Hello, love. Did you get a good night's sleep?"

"I don't know. Why don't you tell me?"

"Don't be hateful, Rose."

"Really? Don't be hateful? How about you leave me alone, and then I won't be hateful," I shouted at his reflection.

"I know what you need. You need to get laid," he stated.

"I would go get laid, if you'd leave me alone," I snapped back.

"I can't let you do that, Rose. I think you'll remember that I don't like to share. But I can help you with your needs," he offered.

I ignored him, then grabbed my robe, and put it on. I removed the towel and began to comb out my hair. After a moment I responded.

"You can't fuck me from in there. Wait a minute. That was you that night, wasn't it? My invisible lover?"

"Yes, it was. How perceptive of you. But I can't do that, now," he confessed.

"Oh, really? And why not?"

"I can't tell you that, Rose. It's my little secret for now. But I can still make you cum. Let me take over your body, and I'll show you."

"How? Every time I let you take over I can't see, or hear anything," I questioned him.

"I'll only take control of your body. You'll see and feel everything that's happening to you. I promise. Don't you trust me, Rose?" Johnny asked.

I didn't trust him at all, but I didn't really have much of a choice either.

"Promise me, you will release control of my body after you've finished with me. Is that agreed?" I asked.

"Yes. You have my word," he promised.

"All, right. Show me what you got."

"Relax, and I'll show you a good time, I promise. Just let me take over now."

I watched as my robe fell to the floor. My long hair was pulled away allowing my full breasts to be fully exposed. My hand slowly slid up from either side of me and alongside my stomach. I trembled at my own touch. But it wasn't my touch after all, it was Johnny's.

I was aware of everything he was doing, but my actions were not my own. Skillfully, my hands grabbed a handful of my breasts, squeezing my nipples until they became hard. Then my hand slowly traced the curve of my neck.

"Oh, how I miss biting that lovely neck of yours, Rose. To be able to taste your blood again," he whispered.

I watched as he pulled a clean razor from the drawer.

"What are you going to do with that, Johnny? Johnny? Please no, don't!" I cried out.

Blood dripped down my chest. My fingers dipped in the warm liquid, placing them in my mouth to taste.

"How, sweet," he whispered.

I could feel the sting on my neck, and then I could feel my hands reach down to my thighs. My pussy throbbed as my clit was teased with moistened fingers. I could feel myself grow hotter under my touch as my pussy was rubbed. A single finger entered me. Sliding in and out, gently, slowly. I sucked in my breath as my insides were explored, just as he used to explore me with his own fingers.

I leaned up against the bathroom counter, as two fingers were inserted into my wet cavity. My breathing was erratic. Fingers plunged into me even harder, the closer my body came to climax. I let out a moan. Johnny always liked it when I was vocal. It turned him on.

"Oh, yeah, Rose. Is that the spot? Are you going to cum for me? Cum for me, like a good little bitch."

"Ahhh, ahhhh, yeah. I'm cumming," I moaned.

I sprayed all over the basin. He always had been able to make me cum that way. I never knew I was a squirter, until the first time we had sex.

As promised, Johnny left me to my own devices after it was over. I put some clothes on and left for the grocery store. At this point, I could have eaten anything, I was so hungry, but I didn't have a lot of cash on me, so I just grabbed a jar of peanut butter, a jar of jelly, and a loaf of bread.

When I went to check out, I was surprised by whom I bumped into.

"Jem. What a surprise? What are you doing here?" I asked.

"I was in the neighborhood. I hadn't heard from you in weeks and hadn't seen you at work, so I was on my way to stop by. I've been worried about you," she said.

"I'm fine. Just been under the weather," I lied.

"Oh, yeah? There's a lot going around right now. What did you have?" Jem questioned.

"Oh, I've had the most unbearable headache. It's like it's taken over my entire body," I answered.

"Watch it, Rose," Johnny whispered in my head.

"So you must be better now if you're out and about. Why don't you finish checking out, and I'll come home with you?" she offered.

"No, Rose. You need to keep that bitch away. You're mine remember?" Johnny threatened.

"I would love the company. I'll meet you in the parking lot. I'm sure I won't be in line much longer," I stated.

"Great. I'll see you in a few then," Jem said smiling.

I watched her leave the store. I looked at the people in line with me.

"Why don't you keep quiet for a change, and let me live my life. Just because you controlled me in life, doesn't mean I'll let you control me in death," I whispered to him.

"I'm warning you, Rose. Don't let her come to our home," he warned.

"Shut up!" I said A little louder than I had meant to.

"Excuse me, miss? Are you addressing me?" The surly woman in front of me asked.

"No, ma'am," I said blushing.

When I finally made it to the checkout, I saw Jem out the window waving at me. I waved back, then took my groceries from the bagger.

I walked out of the store to meet Jem in the parking lot. My stomach knotted up on me. I wasn't sure why. But I had this horrible feeling of dread sweep over me.

CHAPTER 9: THE MISSING

Jem pulled up behind me in the driveway. We both got out of our cars at the same time. She immediately came up to me for a kiss. Without thinking I pulled away from her, and went to unlock the door.

"Is everything ok with you? You seem different. Did I do something to upset you?" she asked.

"No, of course not. I'm just thinking maybe today isn't a good time to visit," I tried to explain.

"Nonsense. Besides, I'm already here."

I opened the front door, and we carried the bags of groceries to the counter. I set my stuff out to make my sandwiches, and Jem waved me aside.

"Go, sit down. I'll make lunch for you," she offered.

"Thanks, Jem," I said, then sat down at the table, and waited for her to bring the food.

"She needs to leave, Rose. This is your last warning to get rid of her," the voice in my head threatened.

I ignored Johnny's warning, and pretended that I didn't hear him.

"Here you go. The best PB&J, you'll ever eat," Jem said with a smile, as she set the plate in front of me.

"Thanks, Jem. You're the best," I responded, as enthusiastically as I possibly could anyway.

"Yeah, well, I try anyway."

We ate our sandwiches quietly. When we finished I cleared the table and put the plates in the sink. When I turned back around, Jem was standing in front of me. She came up to me and pushed some hair behind my ear. Her lips were warm, pressing into mine as she kissed me softly.

"So, what would you like to do now?" she asked softly.

"Well, that was nice," I said, before kissing her again.

Jem had me pinned up against the sink. All of a sudden, I pushed her away.

"What's the matter?" she asked.

The confused expression on her face made me feel horrible. It wasn't me that had pushed her.

"Nothing. I'm just starting to feel a little tired is all, I think my headache is trying to come back."

"How about you let me, help you rid yourself of that headache. I know several pressure points in the hands, neck, and feet that will relieve the pain, before it becomes unbearable."

"Jem, that's really not necessary," I said, trying to come up with some kind of excuse.

"Nonsense. Here, let me try anyway. If it doesn't work I know of other ways to relieve the pressure, so you can relax," she offered again, smiling.

She took my hand in hers, pinching the place between my thumb, and my index finger. Without having control over my body, I yanked my hand from hers.

"Um, ouch! That hurt. I don't think that will work. Maybe I should go and lay down," I stuttered awkwardly.

"Would you like some company? Like I said, I can help you to forget about your headache," she purred.

She pulled me to her and kissed me. I returned her kisses now that I had control again. We slowly walked towards the bedroom while still kissing. I stopped her halfway there for a moment, before we went on to the bedroom. I pulled her down to the black leather couch in the living room, as we continued to explore each other's mouths with eager tongues. Our hands slowly undressed one another, exploring once-familiar flesh.

During our heated union, Johnny interrupted me.

"Do you like that redheaded piece of ass, Rose? I don't think I made myself clear, did I? Get her out, while you still can. Or, I will," he threatened again.

I ignored the jealous man in my head, and I kept my attention on Jem.

We were naked now, our bodies pressing together tightly. I loved hearing the tiny moans escaping her lips. I slid my hand between us, and began to finger her. She rode my hand, and I sucked on one of her pink, erect nipples. Her hands reached under me slipping a finger in me.

I took in a deep breath, then all of a sudden everything changed…

I pushed her down on her back. I grabbed her thighs pulling her closer to me. I buried my face in her crotch, then roughly shoved two fingers into her. I sucked her clit, and finger fucked her forcefully. She began to cum, then I pulled out my fingers and shoved them in her mouth. She sucked her own juices from my fingers, before I pulled her up to turn her around. I slapped her ass hard, she let out a gasp and took it in stride. I pushed my fingers deep inside her again from behind. She was already on all fours, but I pushed her face down into the cushions. I held her there in place shoving my fingers harder and faster inside her, until I felt my hand covered in her wetness.

I pulled my fingers from her, but still held her down into the cushions. She started to move, but I held her firmly now with both hands. Jem started to yell that she couldn't breathe, but I just pushed her face deeper, and then put my full weight against her. She tried to buck me off of her, but I wouldn't budge.

"Please, stop this! Don't make me hurt her!" I cried out.

Jem kept fighting me with all her might, until she started losing consciousness.

"I warned you, Rose. But you didn't listen, did you?" Johnny hissed.

"No! I won't hurt her!" I screamed.

I pulled Jem up from the couch. She gasped for air, as she was finally able to take a breath.

"What the fuck was that? Are you trying to be kinky? I'm not into that crazy shit. Choking is not one of my things. What has gotten into you?" she questioned me, still trying to catch her breath.

"I'm so sorry, Jem. It wasn't me, I swear it," I pleaded with her.

"Then who the fuck was it?" she said glaring at me.

"I don't know. I don't know what came over me just then? I'm really sorry."

I went to her, to try and console her, but she backed away from me.

"I think it's better that I leave now."

"No, wait. Jem, please don't go," I begged.

"I don't know what's gotten into you, but you need to get it out, whatever it is," she scolded.

"Oh, you have no idea," I grabbed her arm, pulling her to me and kissed her on the cheek, "I am sorry. I didn't mean to hurt you."

Tears immediately came to my eyes from the sudden sting across my face. I stood there in shock. Jem looked at her hand.

"I, I didn't mean to hit you. I'm sorry, it was a reflex," she whispered.

"It's ok, I deserved it. I didn't mean to hurt you either," I whispered back.

She kissed me tenderly.

"I can forgive you, if you can forgive me."

"Of course," I said before returning the affection.

"I'll see you at work then?"

"Yes. I'll be back to work as soon as I'm better," I added.

Jem started to dress, and I grabbed the rest of her clothes and threw them at her.

"Hurry up, bitch! Get dressed, and get the fuck out!"

I couldn't control it. It was at that moment when Johnny had taken over completely.

Jem quickly picked up her clothes, crying.

"What the fuck, Rose!"

Johnny used this moment to his advantage, as he used my body as a weapon against someone I cared deeply for. I grabbed Jem by the arm, it didn't matter she was half naked, then dragged her to the door.

She was crying hysterically now. I wasn't there for her, as I cried inwardly for her.

"Please, Rose, why are you doing this?" Jem asked.

I had a brief moment to suppress my mind's parasite.

"Please, help me. It's Johnny. He's back. I can't keep him away much longer. Please, get help," I whispered.

The shocked look on Jem's face was the moment I knew she believed me. She didn't say a word and ran to her car. That was the last time I would ever see my best friend again.

After that day, Johnny never allowed me to have control. I only watched my life through his eyes, as he became me, and I faded into the back of my mind...

CHAPTER 10: THE VISITOR

The next day, my best friend Jem went to Magus for help. He was the High Priest of the coven. He was ,well-versed in paranormal activity. If anyone could help me it, would be him. I knew after my plea for help, and the episode that had occurred the day before, Jem would go straight to our priest.

I no longer had control of my body or had control over my mind. Johnny had me trapped like a prisoner, and it was my body that was the holding cell. He told me I was being punished for disobeying, that if I had listened to him, I wouldn't be in the state I was in right now.

The worst part of my punishment was that Johnny had stopped talking to me. I was completely cut off from anything going on around me. Shrouded in darkness, I could not hear or see anything. My life as I knew it seemed to be over…

Johnny looked at himself in the mirror. The reflection changed repeatedly from his own, and then to mine. When he focused on mine, he proceeded to touch my body.

"Oh, Rose. You've always been such a hot bitch to me. Oh, how I miss fucking you with my former body. I miss your taste and touch upon my body. You were so skillful in the bed."

Johnny reached down, rubbing my pussy with one hand, and a plump breast with the other. The way he pinched my nipple would have caused me great pain, if I'd been allowed to feel it. He shoved my fingers into my pussy as far as they would go.

"You're so wet, Rose. I must taste you," he whispered, then placing my moistened fingers inside my mouth. "Mmm, you taste so nice. Let's see how flexible you are," he said before contorting my body.

I had always been incredibly flexible, but I could never reach my head between my legs.

The sound of joints cracking echoed in the bathroom as my body bent completely forward, and my spine curved even further, so my face could be buried into my own pussy.

He moaned, as he used me to eat myself. My body was propped up on the sink, and my legs were spread out wide to either side of me. Johnny took turns with my tongue and my fingers. Taking his time to explore my pussy fully.

"Oh, I want to feel you squirt on me, Rose. I want to make that little pussy quiver after I'm through with it. Maybe you should be able to feel this one, my love," he said.

I had been allowed to see and feel what was going on. I screamed inside from the intense pain I felt from my body being almost folded flat onto itself. I still had no control over my physical self, only that of my vision and my sensory receptors, so that I could feel everything he was making my body do. I was helpless to fight him.

I felt myself nearing climax, and Johnny could tell from my trembling.

"Oh, Rose, yes. I want you to cum for me. That's a girl. I want you to squirt all over me."

My body betrayed me, and it was the most bazaar feeling eating my own pussy, and feeling myself cum onto my own face. Johnny made me stand up, it hurt so badly. It was as though I had broken bones.

"What's the matter? Did you not enjoy that, Rose? I did it for us. It's the only way we can truly be together as one. And after I complete the spell, we will be," he questioned me with a smirk.

Then he was interrupted by a knock at the door.

"Looks like we have company. I think it's our priest. Let's go find out, shall we?"

We left the bathroom to look through the peephole in the front door. It was Magus. I knew he wouldn't leave until I opened the door.

"Go ahead, Rose, let him in," Johnny coaxed.

Then it was as if Johnny stepped aside to allow my soul to take control of the steering wheel, after he had been in control of driving for so long. I turned the knob and opened it slowly.

"Hello, Rose. How are you feeling? Jem said you've been a little under the weather," Magus asked, smiling at me.

"Yes, I was. But I'm better now. Would you like to come in?" I asked, stepping aside so he could enter the house.

"I like what you've done with the place, it looks nice."

The door slammed shut behind us.

I motioned for Magus to join me on the couch.

"Please, come and sit. What do I owe to the pleasure of your visit?"

"To be honest, Rose I'm here because Jem called me, worried about you. She said you've been under a lot of stress lately, and out of control. Then her phone cut out before she could say anything else. Then later I found out she was in a terrible car accident," he stated.

"What? How did that happen?" I asked almost in tears.

"Apparently, her car flipped over and burst into flames. By the time the fireman arrived, it was too late. I'm so sorry to bring you such bad news. But do you know what she was talking about? Why was she so upset over yesterday?"

I had to be careful how I answered him. Johnny was always

listening.

"I had a horrible migraine come up on me all of a sudden yesterday. I blanked out from the pain inside me. I can't believe Jem is gone. She must have been so scared by my actions," I added.

"Careful, Rose. I can take over at any moment. You don't want me to hurt him too, do you?" Johnny interrupted.

I ignored him.

"I just want you to know the coven and I are here for you if you need us for anything," the priest offered.

"Thank you, Magus. But I'm fine, really. There's no need to worry about me. Do you know when the funeral will be held?" I questioned.

"I'm not sure actually. Even though she was a Pagan, her family was Christian. So I'm not sure if I will be the one presiding over the funeral, or not. You're coming either way, aren't you?" he asked.

"Yes, I will try. I've been really busy. My life is out of control right now," I said, wiping the tears from my eyes.

Magus looked at me strangely with his hazel eyes. His eyes seemed to offer so much wisdom, and his heart much kindness when he smiled at me.

"Loss has its brutal effects on all of us at some point in our lives. I know it's been hard on you with losing, Johnny, and now losing, Jem. Just know I'm here for you," Magus said placing his hand on my knee.

The warmth of his hand caused me to pull away.

"I'm fine. It was hard to get over the pain of losing, Johnny. But I'm dealing with it every day," I admitted.

"Are you still having trouble getting over him? Are you allowing him to be part of your life, instead of letting him go?" he said, leaning in closer to me.

He wrapped a strong arm across my shoulders.

"I have to deal with it, yes. I tried to move on with Jem, but the past wouldn't allow me to. If you get my meaning."

"You're having difficulty moving away from Johnny's memory. I understand, and it's perfectly natural. There are some exercises I can help you with. Come closer, and close your eyes," he directed.

I hesitantly closed my eyes. Johnny was being too quiet in my head.

"Now, I want you to focus on his image. Concentrate on Johnny, focus that energy to let him go," Magus said, taking my hands into his.

"Tsk, tsk, tsk, Rose. I warned you. He's trying to make me leave. Don't listen to him. I won't let him break us apart," Johnny interrupted.

"No," I muttered.

"It's going to be ok, Rose. Let him go. You can't let his memory keep you from moving on with your life," Magus coaxed.

"I know. But I love him so much that it hurts," I said, then began to cry again. These next words were not my own and forced out of me.

"I'm sorry. Will you excuse me? This is all too much for me right now."

"Of course, my dear. Take your time. I'll be right here, if you need me," he offered.

Johnny walked us into the bathroom.

"What the actual fuck is the matter with you, Rose? I thought you loved me? I thought we were going to be together forever?"

„Johnny, please. I can't take this anymore. You're out of control. And what did you mean by you'd hurt Magus too. Did you hurt Jem? Did you cause the accident somehow?" I said, leaning into the mirror at his reflection.

"Of course not, Rose. You heard him, it was an accident.

You believe me, don't you?" Johnny asked.

"No, I don't. I don't trust you at all. I've not in a long time, even before the accident," I stated bravely.

"Trust this, Rose. If anyone gets in our way of being together forever, I will stop them," he threatened.

"Stop them how?"

"You'll see."

I turned away from the mirror and ran back to Magus for help, but it was too late. I clenched my stomach and fell to the floor. The pain was unbearable, and I began to scream…

Magus jumped upon hearing my screams. He ran towards the bedroom and stopped dead in his tracks when he entered the room. Floating slowly above the covers, I plunged my fingers uncontrollably deep into my pussy. My dark brown eyes rolled to the back of my head, and I had begun to spin around slowly, until rotating back to face Magus. He was standing in the far corner of the room motionless.

"I need a young priest, and an old priest, so I can fuck them both at the same time," the voice hissed, and then burst into maniacal laughter. Fingers still plunged even harder, and faster into my swollen pussy. It was at that moment when my head went back, my body contracted, and then I came, squirting all over Magus.

"Who, are you?" Magus asked, wiping the cum from his bearded face.

"I'm surprised you don't know your old apprentice," Johnny said.

"How could you have done this to her?" Magus questioned.

"I'd been preparing for this moment long before my death. You should know. You taught me all about how I could come back from the dead. How to haunt someone, and then how to possess someone. I owe it all to you. That's why I won't have to kill you. For now," Johnny stated.

"Please, Johnny. Let, Rose go. She's innocent. She's done nothing to you."

"You're right, she is. But I love her, and I'll be with her forever, even in death. I will never release her."

"I will not let you harm her anymore. I will stop you from this madness. You must move on and let her go. If you truly love her, you will. Take me instead, if you must," Magus offered.

"I will never let her go. Yet, I find it oddly amusing that you would offer up yourself in her stead," Johnny said, then waved his hand, sending Magus up against the wall. Johnny quickly walked over to his former mentor, taking hold of Magus's throat and lifting him up from the floor.

"I'm warning you now, priest. Stay out of this, and I'll let you live. Interfere, and it will be the last thing you do. I'd hate for you to have an accident too," Johnny warned him.

Magus fell to the floor when his throat was released. The priest got up slowly, keeping a close eye on Johnny.

"I won't let you hurt her, if it's the last thing I do in this world," he said on his way out the door.

The High Priest left and went straight home to gather his coven. He'd made several calls to each one of his thirteen coven members, telling him to meet him later that night at Rose's house. Magus didn't want to wait much longer, but he knew if he returned tonight, it would hopefully catch Johnny off guard.

CHAPTER 11: THE VANQUISH

Later that night all thirteen-coven members joined Magus outside of my house. They linked hands, and Magus led them to the door. It opened on its own as he reached for the doorknob…

The coven entered the house cautiously. The lights were flickering, and the room was cold.

"We need to stay together as a group. Johnny's spirit is strong, and he will not allow us to vanquish him easily," Magus said.

The entire house went dark.

"I need you all to start chanting now. I'll spread the salt," the priest stated.

Magus opened the container of salt, but before he could pour it onto the floor in front of them, it was knocked out of his hands.

"Do you think salt will stop me? I'm no demon, Magus. I am but a wayward soul trying to keep a hold in this world, and the only way I'll leave is when I let go. I'll never let go, Magus, and you can't force me either. You should know that. After all, it was you who taught me how I could remain here," Johnny laughed.

"Show yourself, Johnny. Don't hide in the shadows," Magus

said.

Johnny emerged from the darkness, as the lights came flickering on. He took over, pushing me to the deepest parts of my mind. I could not use any of my senses, and I had no idea what was going on.

Magus looked at the frail shell before him, I was no longer what I used to be. My body was no longer voluptuous, it was thin and frail. My skin no longer had a pink glow, it was sullen and pale now. The fresh beautiful glow around my cheerful dark brown eyes was now sullen with dark circles. My shiny, healthy long black hair, was now a dull, lifeless, matted mess. I was no longer the person he knew me to be.

"I'm not afraid of you, or your coven, Magus," Johnny stated in his voice.

Magus began to chant, then the coven joined him, casting their spell in Latin, while trying to expel this evil from my body.

Johnny stood his ground from within my body, staring them all down, as he smiled wickedly. The wet splattering sound distracted Magus for a moment, when he looked to the floor at my feet, he saw that I had pissed all over the hardwood floor. Suddenly the lights went out.

"Let's stay together everyone. This is what he wants," Magus said.

When the lights flickered back on, Johnny had vanished. Magus took a few steps forward, but then was pushed back into a few of the other coven members, still standing in circle formation.

The front door opened behind them, and Johnny appeared again before them.

"You cannot vanquish me!" He shouted, then waved his hands forward, sending all the coven members out of the house. He countered with his own spell also in Latin, cursing all of them, as he slammed the door closed.

Magus scrabbled to his feet, helping the others to theirs.

"We must stay together. He is trying to separate us with fear. Don't let him. Let us join hands. Focus your energies in unison, to call him to us from out of her body. If we can't banish him, then we'll have to summon him," Magus instructed.

The coven joined him in a circle, seated just outside the door, chanting once again. They swayed side to side in unison, creating the cone of power. It couldn't be seen by the naked eye, but the energy could be felt rising up above them and within their circle.

It was all they could do, to try and save me…

The coven continued to chant into the early morning hours, but they couldn't call Johnny's spirit to them. Magus was exhausted, but he didn't want to give up. He saw the coven was tired as well; their voices were raspy and almost gone.

"We must stop now," he said, breaking up their chanting. "Go on home, all of you. I'll call you when I've derived a new plan to banish him from Rose's body. You all must go home, and rest. Tomorrow will come early, and we will need all of our strength combined, to rid him once, and for all," Magus said, determined to save me.

While the coven members retreated to their cars, Magus looked up towards the house. He saw me standing in the window. Even though he knew it was Johnny in control of my body, he wasn't giving up on trying to save me. Magus knew I was in there somewhere. He just needed to find a way to get me out…

CHAPTER 12: THE PLAGUE

Later on, as one of the female coven members had left my house, a deer in the road startled her. She tried swerving to not hit it. The car skidded across the road and flipped over several times. The woman tried unfastening her seatbelt, but it wouldn't budge. She started to panic, screaming for someone to help her. Flames engulfed the car, filling it with smoke, as she poured with sweat and gasped for air.

Neighbors a few miles up the road heard a loud explosion, and by the time the fireman arrived on the scene, it was too late…

Magus watched as reports of tragic car accidents swept over the news. One by one, his coven members died in the same manner as Johnny had. There was nothing, Magus could do to stop it.

The High Priest had to work fast, before Johnny hurt anyone else, including himself. Magus had hoped that Rose would find the charm bracelet he dropped in her house, during the attempted vanquish. It was his mother's, and it had a protection stone encased in one of the charms. If Rose picked it up and put it on, it would break the hold Johnny had on her, allowing her to have control again, but for only a short period of time…

The television came on in the living room and stirred me to consciousness. I opened my eyes and looked around the room, then I looked at the television screen for a few minutes. The news was on. The reporter was saying how several prominent members of a local coven were found dead, from car accidents. I stood up and ran into the bathroom.

"Why did you show this to me?"

There was nothing, but silence.

"Tell me, Johnny. What did you do to those innocent people?" I questioned.

"They weren't innocent, Rose. They were trying to break us apart," Johnny stated.

"They were only trying to save me, from you."

The slap across my face came hard, and fast. Tears welled up in my eyes.

"Why are you doing this to me? Why won't you just leave me be?"

I ran back into the living room. I tried to open the front door, but it wouldn't.

"You can't keep me here!" I shouted.

"Yes, I can, Rose. Until you learn to love me the way you used to, I'm afraid I have no other choice," he said.

"Or, what? You'll kill me, like you have all the others? They were the closest people to family that I had," I pleaded.

"I'm sorry, Rose. You and I are family, just as we've always been. Those people weren't your true family."

"You killed Jem too, didn't you?"

"She was going to take you away from me. I had to kill her too. I planted a hex bag in her clothes when I threw them at her. Don't you see, Rose? We're meant to be together for all eternity," Johnny declared.

I fell to my knees. There had to be another way of escape from him. While I was on the floor, I spied something shiny under the couch. I crawled over to the couch and reached for it.

My Love Inside Me

It was a charm bracelet.

"What do you have in your hand, Rose?"

"It's the charm bracelet that I've been missing for some time," I whispered.

"It's pretty. Why don't you try it on?"

When I pushed the clasp together, I felt different. I couldn't hear the voice in my head; I could think and feel on my own. I wasn't sure how long I would have control of my body, so that's when I made my decision. I ran to the phone as quickly as possible.

"Magus, hi. It's, Rose. I found the bracelet. How soon can you get here?"

I hung up the phone, and waited...

CHAPTER 13: THE AWARENESS

In the moments after I'd found the charm bracelet, my life seemed to be back to normal. I knew this would only be temporary if I didn't banish Johnny from me soon. When I saw Magus pull up, I ran to the door. This was my chance to finally rid myself of my parasite for good.

"Rose. It's so good to see you. How are you holding up?" Magus asked softly.

"Not bad I suppose, for being possessed by my dead boyfriend anyway," I said, trying to make light of the situation.

"We don't have enough time to act. But, there's something I need to tell you."

"What is it? We can do this now, can't we?" I questioned fearfully.

"I'm afraid it's going to be up to you, to banish him on your own. If I try to do it, he can block my magic. He won't think you'll be strong enough to expel him. I taught my old apprentice well. Maybe too well, unfortunately," Magus confessed.

"What did you mean by your old apprentice?"

"I took him under my wing after he'd had a run-in with some friends who practiced the dark arts. Of course, this was before he met you, but he did have a dark past."

"How dark?" I asked, almost in a whisper.

"The group he was with used sacrifices, to call the spirits from the other side. They would use them to make their spells stronger, then in turn, became more powerful. However, they weren't aware that these spirits could possess them, until it was too late. Many members of the group became possessed and ended up taking their own lives, to finally be rid of the spirit inside them. Johnny had become possessed too, but somehow he used the entity to his advantage. He became very powerful, using the spirit's powers for personal gain. But what he didn't realize, was that a price had to be paid as well. He met me through a mutual friend, who'd told him that I could vanquish the spirit for good. Johnny was on the brink of insanity by the time I met him. I helped him to banish the spirit, and then taught him how to prevent it from taking him again. After that, he became obsessed with the paranormal, then I made him my apprentice. I taught him everything I know," Magus explained.

"That would explain what he's been working on in secret," I surmised.

"What do you mean?"

"He wouldn't tell me anything, except that it was a spell to keep us together forever. Does that make sense to you?"

"He's trying to merge the souls," he stated.

"What is that?"

"The merging of the souls is where he will try and fuse his soul with yours. It would link the both of you forever."

"Oh, my. How do we stop him?" I asked, fearful of his answer.

"We may not be able to. These killings are a part of the sacrifices he had to make for the spell to work. Thirteen by fire, and one bound by love. Your friend Jem, loved you, which made her the one bound by love. These sacrifices, had to be those in your life who were the closest to you. There's only one way to stop him before it's too late," Magus said.

"Please tell me. I will do anything to prevent having to be

stuck with him for all of eternity," I begged.

"It will have to be a bloodletting spell, something strong enough to banish him for good. It will finally send his spirit home to rest. I will write down what you'll have to do. I can't take the chance in telling you in case he surfaces and overhears us. This will be your only hope in setting yourself free of him," he added.

"I'll do whatever it takes."

Magus left me alone to gather the provisions on the list. I had to go into town for a few of the herbs that I didn't have in the cabinet. I had to hurry. Magus had also written on the note, that the charm could only keep Johnny at bay for so long.

Depending on how powerful he was, he would find a way sooner or later to make contact again. If he did, it would only be a matter of time, before he could take control of me once again…

CHAPTER 14: THE BETRAYAL

Long after Magus left, I had gone to the local herb store to get some fresh mandrake root and some belladonna. I had most of the provisions on the list that my High Priest had given to me for the banishment spell. I only had a short period of time, before Johnny could break through the power of the protection charm. It was up to me alone to work fast, in order to work the spell in time to finally be rid of him for good.

While I was searching for a brand new black candle for the altar, I came across a wooden box in the far back corner of the closet. There were strange markings on the box. I wiped away the dust, revealing protection symbols. Which meant something very important was in that box. I tried opening it, but it seemed to be glued shut. Without having anything sharp on my person, I took it into the kitchen to find something in there.

Once I set the box on the counter, I looked in the drawer. The sharp knife I'd found cut through the glued-down edges of the box with ease. When I opened the box, I immediately stepped back, covering my mouth with my hand. Tears welled up in my eyes before I could look away. How could Johnny have done this?

Anger replaced fear and betrayal, then I went back to the

bedroom closet to dig deeper, to find out what other secrets were hidden. I stripped the closet of Johnny's clothes, throwing them all over the room.

When I reached the back of the closet where I had found the box, there was a panel from the wall sticking out. I pulled it off and discovered a small hole. I reached inside, pulling out a book and a liquid-filled jar. Then I reached back inside the hole to see if there was anything else, and I retrieved several tiny sacks filled with herbs.

The jar from the hole had a man's left hand inside. The book was covered with protection symbols, but strangely not covered in dust. A page was marked with a red ribbon, so I opened the book there. This was Johnny's grimoire, it had to be. The marked page was that of a spell to unite one's spirits together. If done correctly, it would link them together for all of eternity. I skipped down and read the ingredients needed.

I slammed the book closed and took it into the kitchen. After observing the contents of the box once more, I knew what it had to have been used for. The deaths of those thirteen closest to me, and the death of a new love were on the list of needed items.

I sat on the kitchen floor wiping the tears off my face. I had to keep my shit together. If I faltered, and allowed myself to become weak, then he had more power over me. I had to get my ass up out of this floor, stop feeling sorry for myself, and get to work on the banishing spell.

Standing before the altar, I had gathered all of my provisions for the spell. I blended the ingredients in my mortar, then rubbed on the essential oils to anoint my black candle. Johnny's portrait was the last to prepare for the spell. I removed the photo from its frame and laid it flat on the table. I sprinkled the herbs and a few drops of the essential oils onto the photo.

The wick on the candle glowed bright red, then burst into flame. I lifted the photo and chanted these words.

"Love of mine, you are no more. Leave me now, in space and time."

I picked up the photo to hold over the candle, when a voice began to call on me.

"Rose. What are you doing, Rose?"

I ignored him. I continued with the ritual before he tried to stop me.

"Rose! If you finish that spell, you only set me free from you. I'll still have more than enough power to kill the others you care so much about," Johnny threatened.

"Oh, yeah? What about all the others you've already killed? I'm not going to let you kill anyone else," I promised.

I laid the photo over the flame, but before it caught fire, my hand went numb.

"I'm stronger than you. You can't fight me, or banish me, as you would like. I'm here to stay."

My hand dropped the photo and grabbed the bracelet from my wrist. The bracelet broke in half, sending the individual charms to scatter all over the floor. I tried to grab the protection stone, but I was too late. The stone rolled down into the open floor vent.

Helplessly, my body was flung across the room. I hit the far wall and crumpled to the floor. I tried to stand up, but I couldn't move.

"Here, let me help you to your feet," Johnny offered.

My body was made to stand up, and now walked to the bathroom.

"What are you going to do to me?" I asked fearfully.

"I'm not going to do it, you are. You're going to finish what I started for me. But first, you need something from the bathroom."

The body, which betrayed me, opened the cabinet door and pulled out a razor blade.

"What are you going to do with that?"

"Now, Rose. Are you telling me that you've not figured all this out yet?" Johnny questioned.

"I don't know what you mean?" I asked crying.

I took the razor with me and walked to the kitchen. I grabbed the box and the grimoire.

"Have you figured it out yet, Rose?"

"What happened to that little girl, Johnny? What did you do with the rest of her body?"

I reached in, pulling the tiny girl's severed hand from the box, and then held it up to my face.

"Before, or after I took her life, Rose?"

"You, bastard! I trusted you. And this entire time we were together has been a lie!" I shouted.

"I never lied to you. I simply avoided the truth. Did you want to know what I did to the little girl?" Johnny asked.

"No, I don't! You sick fuck!"

"Oh, I'm sure you want to be fucked too, don't you? I may work something out for you. But right now, we're going to work a different kind of magic," he stated.

Johnny walked us to the altar. He raked my arm across the table, spilling everything to the floor, all but the lit black candle. He set up his grimoire, then set out the dead girl's hand on the table. He reached under the table and popped up a hidden drawer. He pulled out pieces of hair from several envelopes and placed them into the cauldron.

"Whose hairs are those?" I whispered.

"These used to belong to the coven members, and from your dead girlfriend. It took me years to acquire the hair from everyone, but I knew this wasn't going to be the easiest spell to work either," he confessed.

He placed a photo of us in the cauldron, and then rolled up my sleeve.

My Love Inside Me

"What are you going to do to me?"

"Blood must be spilled, my love."

"Don't you think enough blood has been spilled?"

"Everyone's, but yours. Here, hold still. Oh, wait you are. I know this won't hurt me, but I'm sure you're going to feel it," Johnny told me.

"Wait! No! Stop!" I pleaded with him.

I screamed with no voice. No one could hear my cries, no one but Johnny. I cried out in pain, tears fell from my eyes, even without controlling them. The warm blood spilled from my arm, as it was slashed open from my wrist to the inside of my elbow.

"You're not afraid of a little bloodletting, are you?"

"If you don't stop letting me bleed out, I'll die!"

"Now, I'm surprised you've not figured out how this spell works. Your spirit must be released from your body, so we can be together forever. Don't you want us to be together forever, Rose?" Johnny asked.

"No, I don't!" I shouted.

I felt the sting of the blade on my other arm; blood flowed freely into the cauldron once more, and I was beginning to feel weak.

"You have no choice, Rose."

CHAPTER 15: THE RESCUE

Magus had tried to call me, but when I didn't pick up the phone by the third try, he left for my house. When he arrived, dark ominous clouds cast a shadow of an evil presence in the air.

Magus opened the door slowly and saw me standing on the other side of the room before the altar, while blood was dripping steadily from my frail arms.

I turned around to face him, but he knew in an instant it wasn't me.

"You're too late priest, she's all mine now," Johnny said, from my body in his own voice.

"She's not entirely yours until she dies, and I'm not going to let that happen," Magus stated, then pulled a sachet from his pocket. He threw it all over my body, and Johnny fell to his knees instantly.

Magus pulled some salt from his pocket and poured it on top of my head. He began to chant, but Johnny had become more powerful than their last encounter. He was flung to the other side of the living room. Magus didn't move.

Johnny squeezed my arms, forcing the blood out faster, trying to quicken my death. When his back was turned, Magus jumped him from behind. He poured a vile of potion down my throat. Johnny gagged and screamed. The potion wouldn't vanquish his spirit, but it would keep him subdued for now, until he can allow me to take control of my body again.

When I awakened, I was in my own bed. My arms were wrapped tightly in white bandages, and my clothes were removed. I looked around and found Magus sitting in the chair beside the bed, smiling warmly at me.

"I see you're with us again. How did you sleep?" Magus asked.

I looked at my bandages.

"What happened to me?" I questioned him.

"Don't you remember?"

"Everything is still a blur?"

"Don't worry about it now, you need to rest. Can I get you anything? Some food, water?"

"Yes, please. I'm starving," I announced.

"Ok, then. I'll go into the kitchen and see what I can find," he offered.

I watched Magus leave, and wondered if it was finally over.

A few minutes later, Magus returned from the kitchen with a glass of water and a sandwich.

"I'm sorry about the menu this evening. You seemed to only have peanut butter and jelly," he teased.

I took the plate and water from him. It didn't take long for me to eat the sandwich and down the water.

"Thank you."

"It wasn't that hard to make a sandwich."

"No, I mean it. Thank you for everything. If it weren't for you, I wouldn't be here right now. I'd be lying on the floor, in a pool of my own blood," I said gratefully.

"I couldn't very well let that happen. You're too beautiful to die so young," he said, reaching out to squeeze my hand.

We sat there quietly looking each other in the eyes. His hazel eyes had always been a comfort to me. Magus had this old soul about him, as if he'd been here several times before, but as different people. He was wise beyond his age, and I had great respect for him.

I held his hand for a moment, before a strange feeling came over me. I reached up to cradle my head letting out a sigh.

"Are you all right? You look a little pale," he said, quickly moving beside me on the bed.

I looked up at him and smiled.

"Well, I did just lose a couple pints of blood. I must have gotten a head rush or something," I said, rubbing my throbbing temples.

"It's good to see you've not lost your sense of humor," he said, brushing my hair behind my ear.

I looked Magus in his narrow eyes, his long brown hair cascaded down his back in waves. He was attractive, for an older man, I had never really taken the time to notice the attraction between us.

As if by instinct we leaned in to kiss simultaneously. He took his time, kissing me softly, but with such ardent passion. I looked at him curiously, as to why he suddenly stopped kissing me.

"Rose, I just wanted to tell you, that I wouldn't hurt you. And if you're not ready to do this, I understand."

"Just shut up, and kiss me," I said, grinning from ear to ear.

That was all that was said, and without another minute to spare, our mouths met each other's once again. I felt his hands slide under the covers, to touch my quivering naked flesh. We lay on our sides kissing, while he explored the full length of my body.

We sat up, and I helped him out of his clothes. Magus had a nice build, his body was lean and athletic. It was surprising to me how well-maintained he kept himself. He then climbed under the blankets with me. Our fingers entwined together as he now lay between my legs. The swell of his cock pressed into the soft inside of my thigh. His hands now cupped my breasts, placing tiny kisses all over them, until he trapped one of my nipples in his mouth.

I arched my body up against his hot searing flesh. I longed to feel his cock buried in my pussy, but Magus took his time with me. He left my chest to trail kisses down my stomach, until he reached the warm moist cavern secretly hidden between ivory legs. I felt his tongue separate my inner folds, until he reached the creamy center. A moan escaped my lips, as he expertly inserted his first two fingers into me slowly. He sucked my clit, while he pushed his hand back and forth. It was in no time that I came hard, squirting in his hand. I watched as he lapped up my juices eagerly, and then returned to lick whatever he'd missed from my pussy.

I couldn't wait any longer, and I grabbed the full length of his hard cock to guide it into me. He pulled away smiling at me. He flipped me over on the bed, until I was on top of him. Holding his cock for me like a gentleman, I slowly sat down on it. His cock slid into me easily. Magus pulled me over, to kiss me again. I moved my hips, slowly grinding myself onto him harder. He took both breasts into his hands, kneading them in a circular motion, and then leaned up to suck on one of my rosy nipples.

I sat up on him, riding him back, and forth. Then I raised my pussy slowly up and down his hard shaft. He let out a moan when I fell over back onto him, raising my ass up and down on his cock, rubbing the backside of my pussy. My clit was grinding into his smooth pelvis, then I lost control.

Magus looked deep into my eyes, and I saw that he was going to cum. I reached around and grabbed his balls, to gently tug on them until I felt the wrath of his cock unleash its fury into my pussy. I met his climax, and came so hard I yelled out. His hips were soaked with our combined hot liquids, as we continued to slide our bodies together as one, to finish riding out our sexual high. I leaned over to kiss him full on the mouth, and after the savory kiss, I blacked out.

"So did you like fucking her pussy?" Johnny asked Magus.

The priest pushed my body off of him, and quickly rolled off the bed.

"How long have you had control of her?" Magus inquired.

"Long enough. But I was able to see everything through her eyes. It didn't take you long before you tried to fuck her. Did it, Magus?" Johnny asked.

"I won't let you take her!"

Magus leapt onto my body, pushing it onto the bed.

"Leave her, Johnny. She doesn't love you anymore, and hasn't for a long time. Let her go!"

We wrestled my body on the bed and rolled onto the floor.

"How do you know, how she felt?"

"I've been her coven leader, and High Priest for years. Do you think she wouldn't have ever confided in me before? She told me everything. I saw the marks you left all over her body. She told me how you controlled every aspect of her life. Her work, her friends, she couldn't have a normal life with you. And you know she can't now. So long as you are inside her, she will slowly give up, and will herself to death, all because of you. Do you seriously want that for her? If you truly love her, the way you say you do, you will let her go," Magus said, then reached for the knife in his pants pocket and grabbed my wrist. He cut me open and recited a spell.

"By the blood we unite, by the blood I set you free, by the blood shed this night, so mote it be."

The lights flickered, and the room shook. Magus struggled to his feet and then went to pick up my body. My eyes flew open, and he could see Johnny's cold stare appear.

"You can't have her!" Johnny screamed, taking the knife, then slicing it into Magus's side.

Magus clutched his side and fell to the floor. Johnny started to leave the room, when Magus grabbed an ankle, pulling Johnny to the floor.

"You're not stronger than I am, priest," Johnny hissed.

"Perhaps not, but I am smarter," Magus said, shoving his pentacle from his necklace, onto my naked flesh.

Johnny was temporarily weakened, now I had my last chance to be rid of him forever, as I regained control of my body once again.

"Magus. It's me, Rose. I'm so sorry he hurt you."

"It's going to be all right. We'll perform the ritual together, and you'll be free of him finally," the priest stated.

"No, Magus. We don't have time. Please, you know what you must do," I told him, staring up at him longingly, then I touched his hand that held the knife. "Do it," I begged, pulling his hand to my heart. "Please, Magus, it's the only way. Please, before he comes back, and I lose control again. I don't want to live this way."

"He finished the spirit-to-spirit spell. If I do this, you'll be trapped together with him for all of eternity," Magus said.

"But you can vanquish him once he's out, then my spirit will be finally free. Please, save me from him," I begged him once again, closing my eyes. I didn't want to live anymore, not like this.

Magus raised the knife high and closed his eyes. He paused for a moment, then lowered the knife. He couldn't do it. My eyes popped open, he saw it wasn't me, then drove the knife straight into my heart...

CHAPTER 16: THE INVESTIGATOR ANNA CURRAN

A mysterious woman arrived on the scene the following day. She asked several questions, as if she were a cop or something. My priest gave a statement to her that he'd found my body when he went to check up on me, and then had notified the local sheriff. Other witnesses said that I was just a stripper at a local club called Diamonds & Dolls, and my coworkers said that I'd not shown up to work in weeks.

After the initial comb-through of the premises, the remains of two other victims were found inside the house. One was that of a little girl's severed hand and a man's left hand, which was discovered in a separate jar. The dogs were brought in to assist in the search, which led them to the closet in the bedroom. The dogs barked and dug at the small hole found in the floorboard, in the back of the closet wall.

The officers also found a hidden door that led into another room. Wall to wall, the room contained large shelves full of human remains in jars. There were also several body parts laid on tables that had long since decomposed. The horrible stenches from the room made the K-9s rub their muzzles with their paws.

The sheriff felt that the higher authorities should be called in for this case. Then that's when she showed up, flashing a badge around like she owned the place, but there was something about her I picked up on. I couldn't place what it was exactly, but now that I was a ghost, there wasn't a whole lot that I could do, except watch what was going on. Unless, I could get close enough to this woman to help her with her investigation somehow...

My name is Anna Curran, and I specialize in investigating deaths related to the occult, and or paranormal. The mysterious deaths end up in a folder filed away in a drawer somewhere, while the FBI sit around scratching their heads and calling it a cold case, because they couldn't figure shit out. It was up to me to find out who these killers are, and why they commit such heinous crimes.

I put on the gloves before I entered the house, and looked for the sheriff. I was surprised by his age.

"Sheriff, I'm Agent Curran with the FBI. Someone called my office saying that you needed help with this case," I said, extending my gloved hand.

The sheriff turned to look at me.

"Yeah, well I was told you wouldn't be called until the state troopers finished their investigation?"

"That's usually the case until I'm asked to step in by my boss," I added.

"So you handle the unexplained mysteries, which pop up with a dead body?"

"Yeah, well, that's my specialty. Mystery cases. Who's the victim?"

"The victim's name is Rose Thomas. She was just a stripper without any kind of a background, not even a speeding ticket," the sheriff stated.

"So a good girl, minus the whole stripper thing, ok got it. What have you found so far?" I inquired.

"We found this hidden room with several body parts that

had been sitting here for some time."

"Do you have a list of any missing persons from here and the surrounding counties?"

"I can have my deputy pull up a laundry list of them," he offered.

"Great. Have you had your dogs search the backyard? If there are bodies in here, sheriff, they'll be bodies in the ground," I told him.

"Take the dogs out back, and start digging boys," the sheriff ordered. "You really know your shit, don't you?"

"The moment it falls from my ass, sheriff. Now, if you'll excuse me, I have a case to solve."

As I was leaving for the backyard, the sheriff grabbed my arm.

"Is there a problem, officer?" I said looking into his deep green eyes.

"No, ma'am. But it's my case too. The victims are locals, therefore it places them under my jurisdiction. Is that a problem, detective?"

I gave him a dirty look.

"Fine. Stay out of my way, and do what you're told," I warned.

"Fine," the sheriff said.

We both walked out into the backyard together. The sheriff's deputy ran up to us right away.

"Sir, ma'am, we've discovered the remains of bodies, from the way it looks, the remains are from several different individuals."

The sheriff and I walked to the site of the overturned ground. Several small graves were made to bury each of the victims. This wasn't going to be a quick, open and shut case.

"I hope you packed your bags, detective. Looks like you're going to stay in our neck of the woods for a while. The local inn is really nice, I can have my deputy reserve you a room if you'd like," the sheriff offered.

I nodded my head. There were more important things to worry about, other than a place to stay for the duration I'd be here. If I had my choice, it would not be having to stay here in this redneck town. I gave orders to the coroner as to how to handle the bodies. He'd never had a single murder victim on his hands, let alone ten, or more. This was going to be a long investigation...

I watched the detective from the shadows. I had hoped that my death would look as though Johnny was my killer. He was, in theory. But I knew, as well as Magus did, that it would be only a matter of time before the FBI agent was hot on his trail. The police may want the man who had taken my life, but he still saved me nonetheless. I won't let Magus take the fall for this. Even though he'd cleaned the evidence to erase that he was involved, other than reporting my death, there was still the chance something would be discovered. Traces of hair, fibers, and the autopsy, of course, would show that I'd had sexual relations just hours before I'd died. Luckily, no one knew of our tryst, but Magus and me. Without proof to coincide his whereabouts, he had no other alibi, and with all the present witnesses dead, there was no one else to dispute Magus's involvement.

I won't let my death be unresolved, but I will help the detective uncover the truth about how I really died. If I can hide from Johnny's spirit long enough to assist the federal agent, I can lead her to the real murderer.

I didn't want my friends to die, and I didn't want to lose my own life. But I'm finally free of the torment that my dead boyfriend had caused. I will avenge my friends one way, or another...

CHAPTER 17: ANNA CURRAN, TRACKING THE KILLER

I began my investigation by speaking with a few of the locals in the neighborhood, then went back into the house looking for clues. I went into the victim's bedroom, to search through her personal belongings. I started with her dresser, and it was almost a cliché finding a picture of her boyfriend in the panty drawer.

"Hey, sheriff, who's the guy in the picture with the victim?"

"Oh, that was her fiancé, Johnny Ryan. This is his house actually, Rose moved in with him a few years back."

"What do you mean by 'was' her fiancé? Did they break up, and he left the house with her?" I questioned.

"No, ma'am. Johnny died over six months ago in a terrible car accident. Rose was with him, and barely made it out alive," the sheriff responded.

"Excuse me, sheriff, but we need you to come and look at this," the deputy interrupted.

I looked at the picture again, and after the sheriff was called away, I stuffed it in my pocket. I decided to scratch the fiancé off the top of the murder list, since he died several months prior to the victim's death. So who was it? And where the fuck is the murder weapon?

A few hours later, the coroner's report came in. The sheriff was first to receive it, and then I took it from him.

"Hey now, this is official business I'm reading here. Who do you think you are, snatching it out of my hands?"

"I'm an FBI Agent, and that makes me automatically your fucking superior officer. Now, if you'll please excuse me, I have a coroner's report to read."

I walked into the victim's bedroom again, to read the report. It said that the victim had sexual relations a few hours before the listed time of death. Also, the inflicted knife wound was in close proximity to the victim; meaning the murderer was within incredibly close contact. I sat there on the bed for a few moments, fanning myself with the report, when it came to me. The priest supposedly called in the victim's death, within at least an hour of the murder. So where was he, before he called the police?

"Hey, deputy, I need a ride over to the priest's house. Think you can arrange a ride for me?" I shouted, entering the living room.

"Yes, ma'am. But didn't you drive here yourself?"

"Yeah, but I'm not driving around, when I have a roomful of officers just standing here, eating fucking donuts, and doing absolutely nothing. Now, find me someone that's useless right now, and have them give me a fucking ride already."

One of the new recruits was pointed out and told he was to be my chauffeur while I was in town. I looked the young man over, he must have only been about twenty years old. He was still a baby in comparison to my age. I was almost old enough to be his mother.

"Come on kid, let's go. And wipe those donut crumbs off your face," I scolded.

"Yes, ma'am," the deputy replied.

Magus lived on the other side of town, and when I arrived, he was more than compliant speaking to me again.

"Oh, Detective Curran, what a nice surprise? Please come in. How can I help you? Do you have any more leads on Rose's murder?" he said, as I entered the house.

"Thank you, Mr. Blain."

"Oh, please, call me Magus."

The young officer tried to follow me into the house.

"You go, sit in the car, and wait on me. I won't be long here," I ordered.

I shut the door behind me, and Magus extended his hand by the sofa.

"Please, have a seat, detective," the priest offered.

I joined him on the couch and looked around the room.

"You have an interesting décor, Magus. It must be in regard to your way of life," I said, trying to be polite.

"Thank you. I love having representations of the different aspects of the Pagan faith, to put it mildly. But I'm sure you're not here to discuss my various pentacles, and deities, adorning my walls, are you?"

"No, I'm afraid not. I reviewed a copy of the coroner's report, and it just doesn't make sense to me. Because it doesn't match up with the time you called and reported the victim's death," I inquired.

"I don't understand, what you're trying to say?"

"The report showed that the victim had sexual relations, prior to her death, like within hours of each other. And her fiancé is dead, so I know it couldn't have been him. So that just leaves you, because you're the last individual she'd had contact with," I informed him.

"You think I had sex with her? She was one of my coven members, and I don't have that kind of relation with anyone in the coven," Magus stated.

"Let me get this straight. You're in a coven of practicing

witches, and you don't have sex with any of your members?"

"That is correct."

"So, no group orgies, or sex magic of any kind?"

"Um, no. I don't convene my coven in that manner. Is there anything else you'd like to know about this case? Because I would really like to know who killed my friend, and all of the other members of my coven. I do hope, that it would be better to find the murderer out there, instead of being here asking about group sex magic," he said standing up, then walking towards the door.

"I do apologize, I wasn't trying to offend you, I'm just trying to get the facts straight," I said, meeting him at the door.

"I gave you the facts, and told you everything I know. Will there be any other questions, Detective?"

"Yes, actually. Where were you, before calling in the murder?"

Magus wiped the sweat from his brow.

"I already answered that when you interviewed me the first time. I told you that I had a missed call, and a message from Rose, to call her back, that she needed to talk. When I called back, she never answered her phone. I got worried after several times trying to call, and at that point, I had decided to go to her house," he stated.

"Even though she lived all the way across town? That's a good thirty minutes away. Do you do that for all your coven members?" I interrogated.

"Yes, I do if they need me, and Rose sounded like she really needed me."

"Do you still have the message she left on your answering service?"

"No, I don't. I deleted it after I heard it," Magus said.

"Why would you delete that kind of a message?"

"Why would I need to keep it, if I'd listened to it already?"

"Ok, so the message is gone. What did you see when you

arrived at her house?"

"Like I stated in the report, I found her in the bedroom when I arrived," he answered.

"Do you make a point in just letting yourself into people's houses, and going straight to their bedroom?" I asked.

"I did knock on the door first, and when she didn't answer, I tried the door. It wasn't locked, so I went on inside, when I called her name Rose didn't answer, I searched the house for her," Magus explained.

"And that's when you found her on the floor, bloody, and a mess, with a knife sticking up out of her chest. Am I right so far?" I pressed on.

"Yes. That's exactly how I found her. Is there anything else? It's getting late, I had plans tonight with the TV, and a good beer," he added.

The frustrated look on his face was what I wanted, to see if he'd crack. But, he seemed too cut, and dry. His story was too perfect, and he just made it to number one, on my shit list.

"Ok, I'll leave you to it then. Have a good evening, Mr. Blain."

"Goodnight, detective."

I watched his house, as we drove off in the squad car. I had the kid deputy drop me off near my room, at the town inn called Lincoln's; it was fitting, and named after the town. My room was on the top floor, the building had only two floors, and it had a full kitchen downstairs. It was your basic mom and pop, bed-n-breakfast, with wall-to-wall, ugly-ass floral wallpaper, but it was quaint. I settled into the room, bringing up a few bags from the car, before covering it up with the canvas. I never liked my car out in the open, for fear someone would fuck it up, knowing it was mine. I can be a real bitch most of the time, and I don't make any friends when I come into town.

Rose Marie Machario

I set my bags down on the queen size bed, my paperwork on the small desk in the corner, and then sat myself on the small loveseat, on the other side of the bed, in front of the old box television. The remote was conveniently located on the arm of the small couch, and I turned it on, just to have some background noise. I pulled out the picture of the happy couple and set it beside me on the couch, staring at it for a few moments, before my vision began to blur. I rubbed my eyes and got up to go to the bathroom. I passed a small refrigerator, that had a microwave on top, which would serve its purpose to keep my liquor cold, and heat up all the TV-dinners, that I'd be eating. I couldn't imagine if this town even has a liquor store or not, so I'm glad to have packed my own bottle, but it would be nice to have a store in town, for when I run out. I took a piss and washed up in the sink, because I was too tired to stand up long enough for a shower. So I stripped off my clothes and hit the sack. I patiently waited for sleep to come, but the fucking water dripping, was getting on my goddamn nerves, so I got up to turn off the water, but it kept dripping. After pulling the door closed, to block the annoying sound, I went back to bed. Finally, there was silence.

CHAPTER 18: ANNA CHASING THE GHOST

The next day I returned to the empty house, which was roped off with yellow tape, to try to find more clues that I may have overlooked. While I was looking through the house, the hair on my arms stood up, and my breath floated out in front of me. I knew then, that I wasn't alone.

"Hello. Who's there?"

I walked out of the kitchen and stood next to the altar. My hair blew off my shoulder, and I turned to see who was behind me. No one was there.

"I promise I'm not here to harm you, I'm here to help you," I called out.

I heard a clank and a small thud, then turned around to see what it was. A candle from the altar fell over and rolled off the table onto the floor. I knelt down to pick up the candle, and the floorboard creaked under my feet. After I placed the candle back on the table, my shoelace got caught on the board, untying my shoe. I reached down to remove my shoelace from the board, which was sticking up slightly from the rest of the floor. This piqued my curiosity, since this hardwood floor was perfectly laid out and even everywhere else in the room. I went back into the kitchen to find something to pry the board up with. The clatter of silverware echoed, as I dug through the drawer, and found the perfect bread knife to use.

I returned to the altar, falling to my knees before it, and began to wriggle the knife between the cracks in the floor. It had become a fight with the loose floorboard, as it refused to give. I tried to pry the knife along the side of the board instead, and pushed the handle flat to the floor. The board creaked, and finally gave way enough to pull it up with my fingertips. I set the board beside me and observed the hole in the floor. The contents weren't too surprising in a witch practitioner's home, as I pulled out their book of shadows from under the floor. At first, I believed this to be the victim's book, but as I turned the pages, I came to the knowledge that it was the fiancé's instead. I crossed my legs to relax on the floor. Apparently, I had a lot of reading to do, from the size of this book. By the appearance of the spine and pages, this book was very old, and I'd almost say it was an antique. With each page I turned, I read the most bizarre spells, concoctions, and recipes for disaster. While I was reading, a page began to flutter. I shrugged my shoulders. It must have been the nearby air vent; the heat or air system could have kicked on. The pages began flipping slowly on their own, and then they settled open at a page that was marked with what appeared to be blood. I read the spell on the yellowed page, and it was called 'uniting the souls'. It had all of the requirements for the spell listed on the page beside it. The spell apparently required blood, human blood, and lots of it. I folded the top corner of the page to mark it, and hurried back out to the police car. The young officer who had primarily been my escort around town, was asleep at his desk, so I snatched his keys. Now if I hurry, I may be able to head back to Magus's house and ask him about this spell. He was still my first suspect in the stripper's murder, but this new evidence will either clear him or make him an accomplice.

Magus opened the door to find his favorite agent standing there, with a smile on her face.

"What can I help you with today, detective?"

I let myself in and walked straight to the couch, patting the seat beside me. I pulled the book from my bag and watched Magus's eyes grow wide.

"By the look on your face, I would imagine that you've seen this before?"

Magus walked over to the polyester plaid couch and sat down beside me. He was quiet for a moment, as he took it from me.

"I have seen this book before, but not in a very long time," he said, letting out a sigh.

"Do you know who it belonged to?" I asked.

"Yes. It belonged to me."

He looked at me with such sincerity in his hazel eyes, that I couldn't help but feel uncontrollable empathy towards him.

"What do mean 'belonged'? Is it yours, or not?"

"Yes, this was my book of shadows, but when my apprentice left to become a solitary practitioner, it disappeared. I had always suspected him of taking it, but out of respect for Rose, I never brought it up. This book had been handed down through my family, for several generations. It has spells, and recipes for the sabots inside it, among other things," Magus said.

"What do you mean by, other things?"

"My family had put the knowledge from our ancestors for everything in this book, including magic that would be considered dark, in the wrong hands. Why do you ask?"

I turned the page I had marked in the book.

"I'm concerned about this particular spell. Because it not only calls for human blood as the main ingredient, but lists them in great detail, for instance, the blood from a loved one, and thirteen family members. Sound familiar?"

Magus lowered his head.

"Yes, I'm afraid so."

"Did you perform this spell, Magus?"

His face turned bright red, and his eyes narrowed when he

looked me straight in the eyes.

"No! It was Johnny, he's the one you want. He is the reason Rose and my coven members are all dead," he blurted out.

He stood up and walked over to the other side of the living room to the fireplace, where the statue representing the Goddess Hekate was on the mantle. I watched as he ran his fingers over the statue.

"Are you trying to tell me, Johnny killed Rose and thirteen other people?"

"Yes. I wasn't even supposed to say anything. I made a promise to Rose that I wouldn't jeopardize my life. She didn't want me arrested for her death, since she was the one that had asked me to take her life in the first place."

I couldn't begin to fathom, what I'd just heard.

"What? You killed Rose? I thought you just said Johnny did? For one thing, how does a guy who's been dead for over six months, come back from the dead, and kill people? And for two, what do you mean by, she asked you to kill her? I'm confused," I said.

"I'm not so sure that you'll believe me, if I tell you?" Magus offered.

"Try me. You've got twenty minutes to convince me not to arrest you for murder."

Magus returned to sit next to me on the couch.

"Johnny was my apprentice, after an incident he had with his own coven. They conjured spirits to use in spell work, to make the spell stronger. Several of them became possessed by their lack of ability to release the spirits. It drove most of them to commit suicide, all but Johnny of course. Somehow, he had kept the spirit inside him, trapping it, so he could utilize its power for personal gain. When he could no longer control it, he came looking for me. I exorcized the spirit and banished it back to the otherworld. When he was finally free of it, and regained his strength, he begged me to teach him all that I knew, including my family's secrets," he explained.

"What family secrets?"

"I have necromancers in my family. They have the power to control the dead."

I burst out laughing.

"Necromancers?"

"Yes."

"Ok, carry on," I said, letting out a sigh.

"I was reluctant to teach him how to use the power of necromancy, because it involved dark magic," Magus added.

I leaned back on the arm of the couch.

"What sort of dark magic, are we talking about here?"

"For someone to gain a necromancer's power, they can do one, of two things. The first is to kill someone and eat their heart, to obtain the power, or they must become a spirit themselves and possess a necromancer. Either way, it involves a great deal of bloodshed," he explained further.

I sat back up, and tucked a loose strand of black hair, behind my ear.

"How does someone become a ghost? I mean, how would Johnny have been able to come back, after the accident?"

"He must have done a spell, before his death. I'm afraid that's in the book as well."

I stood up and began to pace his living room floor.

"Ok, let's think about this. Johnny came back as a ghost, then went on a killing spree? And how could he physically kill people, as a ghost? Wouldn't he just pass right through someone?" I asked, afraid of the answer to my stupid questions.

"Not necessarily. Ghosts can move objects, they can make noises, like a whisper, and they can possess people, but only if they're strong enough. He'd had to have cooked up a pretty strong spell, to become that powerful of a spirit, in order to possess another human being," he explained.

I stopped pacing for a moment and looked at Magus.

"Let me guess, it's in that book too? Am I correct?"

"Yes it is, I'm afraid."

"So Johnny comes back as a ghost, possesses some poor bastard, and goes into mass murder mode, to do what? What was the purpose of killing all those people? Let alone, all of the bodies that were dug up from the yard, and the ones found in pieces in the hidden room," I questioned.

I was taken aback, by the surprised look on Magus's face.

"I take it you didn't know, about the other bodies?"

"No, I didn't."

"Did Rose know? She was his fiancé. Where was she, when he was off killing all these people we found in the ground, and in the house?"

"That had to have been before she met him. And she never knew of his dark sorted past. I told her about that. I don't think she believed me at first, possibly from shock, or the fact that he was possessing her at the time," Magus said.

"What do you mean, he was possessing her?"

"Rose was possessed by Johnny. That's why she asked me to take her life. It was the only way she could be rid of him."

"So she killed her best friend, and the other coven members?"

"No, she didn't. Johnny was using her body, as his own. When people are possessed, they have no control over their own actions. The spirit is in control unless they allow the host to have control, but only when they desire them to. I had only a few moments with Rose, in which she had control. Everything else was Johnny," he explained.

"So let me get this straight. Johnny possessed Rose, made her kill people, and then made you kill her, am I tracking so far?"

"Yes, that is correct. Does this mean you're going to take me in, for Rose's murder?"

"I can't without probable cause, or the murder weapon. Right now as it stands, it's a cold case without the proof. And

I can't very well prove, that a dead guy possessed the murder victim, and then made her kill the coven members, now can I? "But I will warn you, once the murder weapon is found, your prints will be all over it. And I'm sure you know what that means," I warned.

"Yes."

I stood up and walked towards the front door.

"I'd better get going. I have much to absorb right now. If I were you, I'd stay in town and find myself a lawyer, just in case."

Magus walked over to the door, then looked into my dark brown eyes.

"Did you not believe anything I just said?"

"Magus, I'm a detective. I believe in the facts. Unless you can prove there are ghosts, that can possess normal, innocent people, then cause them to commit murder, then no, I don't believe you. I'll stay in touch," I said.

I left the house and could feel Magus's eyes upon me, when I got into the borrowed patrol car. I believed in what he said, but I wasn't going to tell him that.

Magus closed the door after the detective drove away. He wasn't going to let the book get out of sight again, took it to his bedroom, placed it into a cabinet, and pulled out a white candle, lit some dragon's blood incense, then locked the cabinet.

Later that night, while Magus slept, an ominous presence crept into the room, like a dense fog rolling into a harbor. His breathing seemed labored, but no one was there to wake him from his obnoxious snoring. The darkness didn't appear to be offended by the sound, as it slowly made its way to the bed, then floated up over the priest's body. Magus took in a deep breath, choking himself awake, then rolled over on his side, before returning to sleep…

CHAPTER 19: THE KILLINGS CONTINUE

The empty liquor bottle lay on the floor beside the bed. A thousand drums were sounding off in my brain, as I wearily opened my eyes. The noise was actually coming from the door. I thought I had placed the do not disturb sign on the door, but apparently, whoever was pounding at the goddamn door, couldn't fucking read.

"Ouch! Fuck!" I shouted, while hopping up and down on one foot.

I looked down to see what I'd stubbed my toe on. It was the liquor bottle. I turned it upside down, and let out a sigh. The door kept pounding, and I heard the sheriff's familiar voice.

"Detective, Curran are you in there?"

"Yes, keep your fucking badge on, I'll be out in a minute," I grumbled.

I staggered into the bathroom and turned on the light, but quickly turned it right back off. I sat down to take a piss, then got up to run through a quick whore bath, however, I took my sweet ass time getting my clothes on. The sheriff could wait a few more minutes. When I put my last shoe on, he was pounding down the door again. I cradled my head in the palm of my hands and grabbed my sunglasses, before I opened the door.

"What the fuck happened to you, detective?"

"Long night with Jack, or was it Jim? I don't remember? What time is it?"

I hadn't even bothered to look at my phone, nor did I remember where I put it. Eh, fuck it.

"It's a quarter after seven," the sheriff said.

"What is so important that you had to get my ass up so early?" I asked.

"Well, I thought you'd be interested in the two new dead bodies that were found in the woods last night."

"Yes, I am, let's go. Any leads, or connection to the present case?"

"I'm pretty sure they are related, by the way they were naked in the woods with their throats slit wide open," he mentioned.

"All righty then, let's go."

The sheriff and I arrived at the crime scene in the woods, by the local park. The couple were there to celebrate the full moon rite and were skyclad, with their throats slit from ear to ear.

"So, detective, do you suppose they're related to the other murders?"

"From the looks of it. There's not a drop of blood spilled on the ground. Did they have any identification on them?"

"Yeah, they live here in town, their names are Bobby and Wilma Russell. You suppose they're part of that coven?" The sheriff asked.

"Possibly. The only way to find out, is to go and ask," I told him.

I knocked on the priest's door several times, before he finally opened the door. Magus looked as though, he had a night similar to my own.

"Can I help you, detective, sheriff?" The priest questioned, rubbing the side of his head.

"Yeah, some more bodies just turned up in the woods last night. Can you tell me where you were?" The sheriff questioned.

"I was here, all night. I went to bed right after you left last night, Detective. I was feeling a bit, run down. Why? What's happened?"

"Don't play like you don't know, it was some more of your coven members that died. To think someone like you would know when your people are dancing naked under the full moon," the sheriff questioned.

"My coven members are allowed to choose when, and where they want to worship. I have no control over what they do, I only guide them," Magus stated.

"I think what the sheriff is trying to say, is that we think another couple from your coven was killed last night. They were sky-clad, and obviously celebrating the full moon rite. The couple's throats had been slit open from ear to ear, and the blood we're guessing had been collected. Do you have any idea what, or who would have collected their blood, and for what?" I questioned.

Magus rubbed his forehead and let out a sigh.

"Are you, ok?"

"Yeah, I've just developed a migraine all of a sudden. Do you know who the couple was?"

"Yes. They were Bobby and Wilma Russell. Did you know them? Where they coven members?"

Magus lowered and shook his head.

"Yeah, I knew them. They were new coven members, for about a month now."

"You mean they joined, even after all the murders?" I asked.

"Yes, they were new in town, so they didn't know. I wasn't going to tell them during initiation, that oh, by the way, my members have a knack for turning up dead. I didn't think that would be a good thing to mention to them. So, let me guess, you think I did this?"

"If it looks like a duck, and quacks like a duck, priest," the sheriff scoffed.

"Hey, that's not called for, sheriff. We have no hard evidence to prove he did it, so lay the fuck off, will you?" I snapped back.

A phone began to ring. Everyone looked to see if it was his, or hers.

"Excuse me, I'll just be a minute," the sheriff said. Then he walked back to his patrol car.

"So, detective, it looks like you had a pretty rough night yourself. You should have stayed a little later, and we could have had a little fun," Magus suggested.

"Let me guess? So you could have had an alibi?"

Magus touched my arm, then gently started to let his hand slide down it affectionately. I pulled away and noticed his eyes looked different somehow. I thought they were hazel, but now they look more like a blue-green in color. He even seemed more self-assured, like an almost kind of arrogance about him. Maybe it was the alcohol from last night, messing with my already throbbing head.

"I didn't mean to offend you, Anna. May I call you Anna? It's such a pretty name," he asked.

"I'm not offended, and it's, Agent Curran to you," I scolded.

The sheriff returned after his phone call, then walked up to me.

"Are you ready to go? I've got shit I need to do, and standing around talking to someone, that we're not going to be arresting, is a waste of my time. After you, detective," the sheriff said.

"Excuse me, sheriff, but it's Agent Curran I do believe," Magus said.

The sheriff stomped off to the patrol car.

I glanced at Magus one last time, before I left with the sheriff. Something was eating at him, I just couldn't make out what that was, but I was hoping he wasn't the one, who killed the couple in the woods.

Magus watched the officers leave, and then went back into the house. He went into the bathroom and looked in the mirror. The water splashed on the counter, as he washed up in the sink and grabbed the towel to dry his face. When he looked back in the mirror, his image became distorted, and changing. He touched his face with shaking fingers.

"Hello, Magus."

"How could this be? I expelled you from her body, you should have moved on?"

"Now, Magus. Why would you think I would've moved on? My love was released to me. We are true equals now. I only need to find her, and then we can truly be together forever. You my friend, are going to help me find her, then perform the ritual. It will be fitting, that you were going to perform the handfasting for Rose and I, now you will truly unite our spirits for eternity," Johnny said.

"No, I won't be doing that for you," Magus assured him, bracing himself on the bathroom counter, and staring down his enemy from the other side of the mirror.

The Druid Priest began to chant the expelling spell in Latin, but Johnny was too strong. The priest fell to the floor, and his body began to convulse uncontrollably. He stopped suddenly, then stood back up to look in the mirror. Johnny's image flashed across the glass before Magus's own image appeared, then he smiled wickedly.

"I'm coming for you, Rose. I made a promise, and I'm going to keep it," Johnny said, before walking out the door.

CHAPTER 20: DIAMONDS & DOLLS

I had the sheriff drop me off at the Diamonds & Dolls club. Of course, he laughed his ass off at me for thinking that I needed a hair of the dog, and wanted to see some pussy. I told him, that I was actually doing my job, by going in and asking some questions. Something was puzzling me, it was the fact, that no one had bothered to speak to anyone at the club.

I walked in, and immediately flashed my badge to the door girl.

"I'd like to speak to your manager, please."

"Yes, ma'am, I'll go ahead and buzz you in," she said.

I walked in and was instantly greeted, by a tall gentleman with a long dark ponytail and beard.

"Hi, I'm David. I'm the manager here. My door girl says you're a cop? How can I help you?"

"I'm with the FBI, actually," I said, flashing my badge. "I'm here to talk about a girl that used to work here, by the name of Rose Thomas."

"Yeah, I was really shocked to hear that she had been murdered. A lot of us here attended the funeral. Have you caught the bastard who did this to her, yet?"

"No, still working on it. That's why I'm here to talk to you, and maybe a few of the other dancers, if that's all right?"

"Yes, of course. We can talk in my office," David offered.

I followed him around the back of the main entrance, where the door girl was. The office was small, with several TVs for video surveillance, all throughout the club. That would answer the question of how he was at the door, to greet me so fast.

"Have a seat, please. What would you like to know? I'll help in any way I can. I adored Gypsy, she was one of my best girls," he said, affectionately.

"Well, that answered my first question. Gypsy, you're referring to Rose, I'm guessing?"

"Yes, Gypsy was Rose's stage name."

"Ok. So how long did she work here? Did she have any enemies?" I inquired.

"She worked here going on nine years now, well it would have been this coming fall. The girl got along with everyone, and any new girls that started working had even respected her."

"So there was no cattiness between the girls?"

"I'm sure Gypsy disliked a few of them, particularly Miller. She didn't care for her much," David said.

"Does this, Miller still work here?"

"Yeah, she's here right now. Would you like to speak with her?"

"Yes. Would it be all right if I used your office, to question a few of the girls? I wouldn't want to draw any attention and alarm the customers, or anything," I asked.

"Oh, yeah, not a problem. I really appreciate the discretion. Many of our customers like to keep their nightlife private, or what they do here around lunchtime during the day. Should I send Miller in first, then anyone else that was close to Gypsy?"

"That would be great, thank you."

When Miller arrived, she seemed nervous, really nervous.

"You don't have to be so nervous, you're not in trouble,"

I said.

"Oh, this isn't about the pot?"

"What pot?"

"The pot I have in my locker. Did someone rat me out?" Miller asked.

"No, miss, I'm a federal agent, and I'm going to ignore what you just said about the marijuana. This is about something else. But if you respect your manager, you won't bring that into the club again. I'd hate for this place to get raided and shut down."

"Yes, ma'am. So what's this all about?"

"I'm sure you're aware, that one of your former co-workers was murdered, right?"

Tears welled up in the young girl's eyes.

"Yes. When I heard Gypsy was killed, I about died. I was so worried about her soul," she said, before losing it.

I passed over a box of tissues, that was on the desk. That manager must need it a lot, because several more boxes were stocked on a shelf, next to the desk.

"Here, wipe your face before your mascara runs," I offered.

"Thank you," Miller sniffled.

"What did you mean by, you were worried about Gypsy's soul?"

"Oh, that since she was murdered her soul might go on to heaven, to be with God."

I rubbed my temples slowly. This was making my hangover worse, than it already was.

"Ok, so what else? Did you hate her? Were you ladies friends?"

"I liked her, sort of. I tried to save her, you know, get her to go to church with me, but she was too big of a sinner to help her," Miller stated.

"What made you think that?" I reluctantly asked.

"Well, I know for a fact what a big whore she was, she fucked both bartenders we had, and had a lesbian relationship with another girl here named Jem."

"I thought she was engaged?"

"Well, she did get engaged to the second bartender we had. His name was Johnny. He was really cool. I felt sorry for Gypsy when he died, all of us girls really liked him," she stated.

"Who was the other bartender, and what happened to him?"

"Oh, he was an asshole, and a pervert. He used to stalk a few of the dancers, and was always trying to sleep with them."

"And you said, Gypsy had sex with him?"

"Well, that's what I'd heard anyway. But if you hear a story around here, it's more than likely the truth," she stated.

I scratched my head and stood up.

"Ok, well I appreciate your time talking with me. You mentioned a girl named Jem, where is she?"

"Oh, she died in a freakish car accident."

"Why would you call it, freakish?"

"Because we had one of the firemen coming in, and he got to drinking and let it slip that her accident was similar to all of those coven members accidents. Serves them right for being heathen witches, I'm glad they burned in flames, just like they will in Hell. But I liked Jem, she was nice to me, even though she was a dike," Miller scoffed.

"Ok, that will be all, send in the next girl," I asked.

I plopped back down in the leather swivel chair, then pressed my forehead to the desk. I sure as fuck hope the next stripper that came in wasn't a bible thumper too. What a contradiction that one was, sheesh.

When the next girl came in, I asked the same round of questions that I did with the last girl. She answered the same way, luckily without all the religious undertones. Then I spoke to the next several strippers, all stating that Gypsy was a great girl, and was always nice to them. They all said they missed her, and had wished she'd not been killed. All the answers were the same, pertaining to Jem, that she and Gypsy were more than friends, and in fact, were lovers. But Jem had died, before Rose did, which automatically scratched her off the list of possible suspects. But some of the girls did mention that Johnny seemed to be very controlling of Rose. That she had to get his permission for everything, even when she worked. He watched her from the bar, while she gave lap dances to customers, and wouldn't stop until the dance was done.

I walked out of the office, and the manager stopped me at the door.

"Were you able to find out what you needed?"

"Yes, for the most part. Hey, let me ask you something. The other bartender, the one that was fired for sexual harassment, a few years back. Where did he go? I'd like to interview him too," I asked.

"Oh, he died right after I hired Johnny on. I kept it to myself, so none of the girls knew. I didn't think they would care anyway. Most of them hated him, well all the girls besides Gypsy. But she got along with everyone."

"How did the bartender die, do you know?"

"Oh, yeah, it was really strange too. He was in his apartment, and somehow managed to hang himself without a rope, or anything. The cops found him in his bed, but the coroner report said that he had hung himself," David explained.

"Let me guess, it was an open and shut case?"

"Yeah, it wasn't but a few days after it had happened, the sheriff dropped the investigation."

"Well, thanks, you've been quite helpful," I said.

"Wait, there is something else you should know," he added.

"Yeah, and what's that?"

"That bartender died the very next day after I had hired Johnny to be the new bartender. I'm not sure if that makes a difference, or not. We all liked Johnny, I felt pretty bad that he died, but I didn't like how he treated Gypsy," David said.

"How so?"

"He was really bossy sometimes, I had to get onto him about manhandling her one night after work. He accused her of being too intimate, with one of the customers during a lap dance. I had to break up their argument, but he apologized and admitted to having been drinking some. After that, I had to let him go. I couldn't have the jealousy with him over her, or the fact he was drinking on the job," he further explained.

"I'll keep that information in mind. Thank you again, David, for your cooperation," I said.

"You're very welcome, and if you'd like, you can stick around and have a drink on me. How's that sound?"

"Well, it is five o'clock. Technically, I'm off duty now. Yeah, I'll take you up on that offer for a drink."

"Cool, go ahead and find yourself a table. I'll send one of the waitresses over with something. What would you like?"

"I'll take whatever, just make it neat."

"Will do."

I began to walk over to a table, when I spotted my favorite suspect, Magus, sitting at a corner table. He immediately saw me and waved me over to join him. Luckily the waitress saw which table I was sitting at and brought my shot to me.

"So, Agent Curran, what brings you to a place like this?"

"I was interviewing some of the dancers, if you must know," I told him.

"Ah, yes, of course. Find anything interesting?"

"Yes, a few things. Did you know about the old bartender that worked here, before Johnny was hired on?"

"Not personally, but Rose confided in me once and told me she fucked him one night after work. She had gotten pretty plowed, and the guy wouldn't stop harassing her until she put out," Magus informed me.

"So, he raped her?"

"No, not necessarily. She fucked him willingly, but it was just because she was desperate, and she wanted him to shut up about it already. She never saw him again, except for one other time outside of work, right after Johnny was hired. But they hadn't started dating yet. However, when Johnny heard about it, he went off and got all kinds of pissed off about it."

"So do you think Johnny killed him?"

"No, I don't think he would have killed him in cold blood. Besides, the coroner's report stated he had committed suicide," he said.

"Really, that's interesting. I've not heard that side of the story yet. What did you think?"

"I thought Johnny was in love with Gypsy, and that's why he was so jealous of the former bartender."

I shook my head after the first shot went down. I let out a breath and set the glass down.

"Would you like another?" he asked, motioning for the waitress.

"Sure, are you buying?"

"Of course. I'll have one, with you," he said, holding up two fingers at the waitress.

I sat back in my seat and began to watch the stage show. One of the girls walked out on stage, booty bouncing to a rap song, and I saw Magus looking objectively at the girl.

"Are you not enjoying the show?" I asked.

"It's just not the same here without Rose. She was the best dancer here, and amazing on the stage, as well as on the pole. No one else could compare to her," Magus sighed.

"I know you must miss her, and I'm sorry you lost her," I said, sincerely.

"I've not truly lost her, I'll find her again, one day."

"Excuse me?"

"I meant in the next life, it's a Pagan thing. You probably wouldn't understand," he said.

"Oh, you'd be surprised how much about Paganism, that I actually know."

"Oh, yeah? Are you a believer?"

"I'm not sure what I believe, but I'll tell you this much. I know what I can see, is believing," I said, as the waitress brought our drinks. "Like this," I said lifting the glass. "A toast, to our old friends that have passed on, may we meet them again someday."

"To old friends," Magus said. "And to our new friends," he added smiling at me.

We clanked our glasses together and tilted our heads back in unison. After a few more glasses, Magus bought me a lap dance, from a young blonde, with perky little tits and a tight round ass. She seemed pretty eager to dance for me, as she grinded her ass in my lap, turning around and rubbing her hard nipples across my face. I liked women, I'd had several occasions where I'd been with a woman sexually, and this dance was making my panties wet. It had been a long time since I was with a woman, and perhaps an equally even longer time, since I'd had sex at all. I was long overdue for a good fucking, and the vibes coming of Magus, made me think he would oblige me.

Magus drove me back to my room, in his 64 1/2 Ford Mustang, and offered to walk me upstairs. As soon as we entered the room and locked the door, our mouths were pressed together and our clothes were ripped off. Hands explored naked flesh, and tongues licked hidden places. I wasn't sure why I was so attracted to him, but I could only rely on my aching loins for answers. He parted my lips with his tongue, as he entered me with nimble fingers. I nearly came all over his hand, as he worked the upper insides of my pussy. I knew he was just teasing me now, as he sucked my clit, and finger fucked me hard. He looked up at me from the floor, as he was nose deep in my crotch, to watch my reaction while he ate me. The fistful of hair I gathered in my hand was soft, as I pulled him up to me. I tasted myself on his tongue for a quick moment, as we stumbled to the bed. He fell back onto the soft mattress, as I followed, then taking his hard cock in my hand and covering it with my mouth. He sucked in his breath, when I swallowed his cock, down my throat. I used my hand to rub up, and down on his shaft, while my other hand cupped his balls gently, to massage them. The way he thrashed about on the bed, was a good indication he's never had his dick sucked so good, so I kept perfect rhythm in my sucking, jerking, and massaging. Then he reached around to play with my wet pussy, as I sucked hard on his big cock. Fingers rapidly went in and out of me, my pussy was so wet and throbbing, that I could barely stand it any longer. I needed his cock inside me. He let out a sigh when I rose up off of him, wiping the spit from my mouth, then I crawled on top of him. Straddling his hips, I held his cock tightly, as I eased my pussy down on top of it. My insides were full of him, as I began to rock back and forth over his hips. Magus grabbed my large tits in his hands, kneading them and pinching my hard strawberry-hued nipples. Hot breath covered a nipple before wetness took over, then his teeth clamped down on one of them. I let out a loud moan, rocking my petite body into his, his thumb found my clit easily, his hand brushing up against my smooth skin. My pussy erupted all over his hips, and down between his ass cheeks, he must have felt me cum, by the size of his smile. Magus grabbed me by the hips, pulling me off of him, then flipped me over onto all fours. He shoved his cock in me, deep wetness surrounded him, as he drove himself hard, his balls bouncing up, and smacking my pussy. I could barely keep my balance, as he continued to thrust his cock inside my wet hole. He grabbed a handful of my long black hair, pulling me up to him, now we were both up on our knees, as he fucked me from behind. Heavy breath fell on my neck; wet kisses made a trail from my ear to my collarbone, and then back to the center. I let out a scream, but he held me tight, as a warm liquid trickled down my shoulder. He licked every drop of blood from my skin, without missing a beat, as he continued to pound my pussy without mercy. I turned to kiss him, and a salty sweetness was exchanged in my mouth, as he returned my kiss. My swollen clit was found once again, as he rubbed it with rough fingers, making me gush all over him, creaming the insides of my pale-skinned thighs. He pushed me down hard onto the bed, and I could barely move, pulling his cock out of my pussy, then cramming it into my ass. A deep throaty moan escaped my bruised lips, and a sharp searing pain hit me unexpectedly, as his cock plunged deeper into my tight ass. My breaths were short, as his full weight pressed against me. His cock moved in and out of me with ease, triggering an interesting sensation, that I'd never been able to enjoy before. A hand reached underneath me, pulling me up on my knees, again working my pussy into a frenzy, as fingers pushed inside my wetness, and a thumb rubbed my clit. I came all over his hand with ease, then he pulled his cock out of my ass and shoved it back into my wet cunt. I moaned at the sensation, as he slowly pulled from one hole, then pushed it back into the other, back and forth, until I lost it.

"Stop with the teasing, and fuck me already!"

He did as I asked, without a word, thrusting hard, yanking me by my wide hips against his. I was lifted up off the mattress with every thrust, as he pulled me into him. He drove his cock into me, harder and faster, then let out a moan when the hot liquid of his cum spilled into my swollen pussy. We both collapsed, breathing heavily next to one another.

I turned to look at him, his eyes were closed. Without disturbing him, I got up and walked into the bathroom, when I came out, he was propped up on his side waiting on me.

"I thought you'd snuck out on me, then I realized we were

back in your room, and not my place," Magus chuckled.

"Well, we both had quite a bit to drink. I don't even think you should have been driving, but I was too fucked up to care," I admitted.

I walked back to the bed and sat down beside him. My fingers combed through his long wavy brown hair. I didn't want to be rude, but I didn't want him to think he was ok to spend the night.

"I don't know about you, but I have to get up early in the morning. I have a case to solve, remember?"

"I suppose that's your subtle hint, that I need to leave?"

"Yes, I'm sorry. I don't do sleepovers. I'm good with getting fucked and all, but I don't do everything else that follows. I hope you understand?" I said.

"Oh, yeah, that's not a problem," he said, sitting up. "I'll get dressed and be on my way."

I stood up and kissed him. After a few moments, I felt his hard cock hitting me on the inside of my thigh. I grew hot again, but it was getting late. I took him in my hand stroking it. Ok, maybe just a quickie. I pushed him over to the chair, and then straddled him, with my feet on either side of him, in the seat. My pussy slid easily on his hard cock, as I bounced up and down on it one last time, until I came, then sent him on his way.

CHAPTER 21: LED ASTRAY

A week had gone by, and I was not only busy with the case, but I was also fucking one of the main suspects. This may prove to be a dangerous liaison, but I had this gut feeling that Magus was innocent. I had been with him every day, and there had been no slip-ups on his end. To think if he were guilty of all the murders, then I would have caught him in a lie, but he never seemed to be different in any way.

I was in my room alone, when the phone rang. It was the coroner's office asking me to come down there. I grabbed my sunglasses and walked out the door. When I arrived, the coroner handed me the lab results that I had been waiting for. I grabbed a chair and sat down. This couldn't be, I didn't want to believe it anyway. I looked at him and tried to keep my mouth shut, but I couldn't.

"Are these the results from the couple that were found in the woods?"

"Yes, ma'am."

"And you're positive, that this hasn't been tampered with?"

"I'm positive, I did all the work myself. These prints were found on both of the bodies and belong to this man. Now, if you'll excuse me, I have more work to do if you'd like to solve your case," he stated.

The coroner walked away and locked himself up in his office. I took the lab results with me and headed back to my room.

My bed was covered with pictures of victims, lab results, a list of suspects, and all the notes I'd taken. The so-called car accidents were labeled just as accidents. They were not only out of her jurisdiction, there was no proof linking the accidents to these new murders, or even to Rose's murder. I separated each photo, with each lab report, then placed them into separate categories. The first category was all the car accidents, including Johnny's. The second category was Rose, she had one all of her own, since it was a stabbing and her blood wasn't taken. The new double murders were the latest ones, and she placed them separately too, as they had throats slit, and blood drained from them, and including it with the new coroner's report. I hugged my knees close to me, and propped my head on my hand, then my eyelids grew heavy...

I sat up suddenly, my shirt was clinging to my skin. I must have fallen asleep. What time was it? I pulled out my cell and looked at the time. It was nearly four, and I had been asleep for the last three hours. What a waste of the day. I had no more leads to go on, besides the papers scattered before me. Then something caught my eye, in the photo of Rose and Johnny. He had a strange tattoo on the inside of his wrist, but I couldn't make it out. It looked like a symbol of some kind. I hadn't entirely dismissed Johnny as the main suspect, but I also couldn't dismiss Magus either. The priest's prints were found all over the couple's bodies, and on their personal possessions. There was enough evidence to arrest him, but I couldn't bring myself to do it. I needed something more to go on, because anyone could place someone else's prints all over a crime scene like that. The question was who? Not to mention there's no motive for Magus to kill his own coven members. My instincts kept telling me that Magus was innocent, or was it my pussy telling me that. I instantly became aroused at the thought of his cock, balls deep in me, but I really needed to focus. I reached down to rub my aching crotch. There had to be proof somewhere that could free Magus from all suspicion. I needed that fucking murder weapon. If I could find the knife, I could track down the real killer. The unfortunate thing was, that the murder weapon had yet to be found. I needed another angle to go on. I needed more evidence. Perhaps, I could go into the evidence room somehow, and see if I couldn't dig up something from the previously buried cases. It was a long shot, but I needed to prove Magus was innocent, not just for him, but for me too.

I left for the sheriff's office, wondering whom I was going to have to sweet-talk into letting me into the evidence room. Then the idea came to mind, and it would work if a certain young officer was working.

As luck would have it, he was there sitting at his desk with a pile of paperwork.

"Hey, there. It's good to see you, officer. How's it going?"

"Oh, hello ma'am. I'm strapped with all this paperwork the sheriff left me since you stole my patrol car," he stated.

"I didn't steal it. I borrowed it. And why did you get into trouble for that? I was the one who took your keys," I admitted.

"Only because, I was asleep at my desk. And that's why, I'm up to my eyeballs in this paperwork," he complained.

"I'm sorry. But I need to ask a favor."

"No, no more favors. You'll just get me into trouble again."

"I promise, I won't tell anyone that you helped me. Please, I really need your help on this. I could make it worth your while," I teased.

I traced the curve of his neck with my fingers and twirled his hair.

"What do you need?"

"I need you to let me into the evidence room."

"What? Oh no, I'm sorry. The sheriff will have me working parking meters if I do that," he stammered.

"I won't tell anyone it was you, that let me in. And I promise, no one will see me go in. Just give me your key. Please?"

"Fine, but you have to promise not to take anything out of there. Just do whatever you need to do, and get out. Understand?"

"Yes. Thank you. You won't regret this. I'll drop your name and say that you helped crack this case, if I find what it is that I'm looking for," I offered.

He reluctantly passed me his card key. I kissed his cheek and took off for the evidence room. I snuck downstairs and saw a guard on duty. I flashed my badge to him.

"Hi, I was told to get you. The sheriff needs something brought down here, but he doesn't have time to do it himself. It's upstairs on his desk," I lied.

"But I'm not supposed to leave my post. Why didn't he send you with the evidence?"

"Because silly, it's my case I'm working on. If I handle the case, and the evidence, it looks as though I'm tampering with it. I'll stay here and watch the door until you get back. Ok?"

"Ok, I suppose I can trust you, since you're a federal agent and all," the guard said.

The guard headed upstairs, following my bullshit tale, so I could enter the evidence room. I slid the card key, and it worked like a charm. I was in…

CHAPTER 22: LOOKING FOR EVIDENCE

I began my search looking for boxes, with the dates of the murders on them. All of the couple's personal belongings were in bags. I saw the rubber gloves on a shelf, and I slipped a pair on. When I opened the bags, the smell of dried blood and patchouli infiltrated my nostrils. My eyes welled up with tears, from the horrible stench, but I couldn't let it bother me. I had to find something. There was no weapon in the box, so apparently it was still missing. All of the clothes were splattered with blood, as if from a distance. If they were naked on purpose in the woods, they would have set their clothes on a tree, or piled on the ground, hence the blood splatters. If their blood was harvested, and the murder weapon was only a medium-sized knife, it could've possibly been another witch using his or her athame. Which would be sacred to him or her, therefore, not leaving it behind, even if they were in a hurry. I placed the evidence back in the box and set it back on the shelf, noticing another box labeled Rose Thomas. I thought it was pretty peculiar that the other evidence box only had the date written on it, and this one had Rose's name on it. I pulled it down and opened it. The box was empty. Could the murder weapon have been in this box? She was found naked at the crime scene, with only a knife inside her chest. It was said that the knife was indeed an athame, Johnny's athame perhaps, or

Rose's. Why would someone remove a possible murder weapon from evidence? I put the lid back on the box and placed it back on its shelf, then I began looking for Johnny's box. The boxes labeled explosions caught my eye. If the cars exploded, what would be left as evidence? When the firemen were never there on time to put out the flames, to save anything. According to Magus, they were able to put the flames out on Johnny's jeep, but not until after the car had exploded. So why would there be a box for him? Only one way to find out, I pulled the box down to find another empty box. This was getting me nowhere, and if I had to guess, these other boxes listed explosions were of the coven members, and of Rose's girlfriend Jem. Of course, any of the remains like teeth or certain metals, could only survive in that kind of a fire. I could understand that the teeth, would be given to family members to place in the ground, but something from the fire would usually be kept as evidence of some kind.

I heard the door open, and then I hurried to place the boxes back on the shelf. It was the sheriff, I was so busted.

"Detective Curran. What are you doing down here? And why did you tell the guard that I had evidence to bring down here. How did you even get in?"

"The guard let me in, I told him you said it was ok. I guess he must have left his post to go and ask you," I lied.

"You still didn't answer my question, of why you're down here in the first place?"

"I was looking for the murder weapon," I confessed.

"That's not been found yet. You know I would call you on something like that, don't you?"

He came closer to me. I could smell his cologne, and the onions on his breath. I had to come up with something better.

"Yes, of course. But don't you find it curious, that the same knife used to kill the stripper was the same size as the one used to slash that couple's throats?"

"Yes, I read the same coroner's report as you did. Now tell

me, what else are you down here looking for," he said, whispering in my ear.

His breath was hot on my neck. I quickly tried to think of another lie.

"I was trying to see if there was a connection to the knife murders, and the car accidents," I said softly.

"Those were just that, accidents, accidents that you have no jurisdiction over, and are completely different cases. Not even real cases, accidents," he chided.

"Then why are there boxes for them in the evidence room?"

The sheriff pushed me up against one of the cages.

"You're a nosy little bitch, aren't you?"

He was nearly a foot taller than I was, but I could still take him down. I had to act fast. Looking into his blue eyes, I had to use my wiles on him, instead of trying to talk my way out of this one because it clearly wasn't going to work on him. My hand reached up to caress the side of his face, he turned his head and grabbed my wrist. His tongue roughly slid along the length of my petite index finger, as he sucked it gently in his mouth. This was going to be too easy.

Our lips met hungrily, our tongues thrusting in and out of each other's mouths. He grabbed my face with his hands, pulling me even deeper into his kiss. I let my hands fall to his trousers unzipping them, reaching inside to find his hard cock. I sucked in my breath when he let me come up for air, as I worked his hard shaft with my hands. He let out a moan, running his fingers down my sides until he grabbed a handful of my round ass through my blue dress trousers. I smiled at him when I pulled his handcuffs from his belt. He instinctively caught my hand with his.

"Don't you trust me?" I asked.

"It depends," he said, smiling.

I removed my right hand from his zipper, and then took both his hands in mine, lifting them above his head, then handcuffing him to the cage. He had a worried look on his face, but I kissed him once more before kneeling in front of him.

I pulled a surprisingly big cock through the hole in his pants, taking him all inside my mouth. I sucked him gently at first, and then I began to two-fist him, wringing his meat in my hands in opposite directions, while I bobbed my head up and down slowly.

The sheriff let out a moan, running his fingers gently through my long black hair.

"I knew from the moment I set my eyes on those petty lips of yours, that you could suck my cock like a champ," he said, with a heavy breath.

I kept bobbing my mouth over him, my hands now holding onto his hips. I masterfully swallowed him hole, my eyes watered, but I never gagged, as I pushed him deep into my throat. The veins on his hard member began to pulsate even harder with the flow of blood. I knew it was time to stop sucking, and start fucking, while I had the chance.

I stood up ignoring the sigh that escaped his lips, then pulled a chair over to hold on to. I left him in the handcuffs and pulled my pants down. He let out a moan as I backed my wet pussy over his cock, sliding down onto his shaft slowly. His cock filled all of my insides, as I slowly raised my body up and down on it. I let out a moan and quickened my pace, backing my ass up into his groin, while holding on to the back of the chair.

"Why don't you release me from these cuffs, and I'll show you what I can really do with this big dick?"

I pulled myself away from him slowly, feeling his cock fall out of my pussy. I turned around to find the key to unlock the handcuffs, and as soon as his hands were free, he grabbed me. He quickly unbuttoned my shirt, and then popped my tits out of my bra, kneading them hard with his hands. His mouth covered my nipples hungrily, sucking the hardened peaks. The air made my wet nipples even harder when he released my breasts from his grasp. Then he lifted up my leg, while the other was left on the floor; he took hold of his wet cock, shoving it back inside me. His hands reached around, pulling my ass hard into his hips, his cock thrusting even deeper inside me. I grabbed hold of the cage as he fucked me hard, then he turned me around, bending me completely over the chair. My hands held the seat of the chair tightly, when he shoved his cock back into my pussy, I held myself up, my hips pressing into the metal back of the folding chair. The chair began to scoot across the floor, until the table stopped it. He withdrew from me and pushed me onto my back on the large table. He pulled my pants off the other leg, and then pulled me by my hips, to line my pussy up perfectly with his eager hard member. I took his sticky wet cock in my hand, inserting it into my swollen cunt. He pushed it the rest of the way slowly, while leaning over to nibble on my neck. Then he took my hands in his and raised them above my head. I never noticed it earlier, but the tattoo on his wrist looked interestingly familiar, but the thought left my mind, as he fucked my brains out on the big white table. He then placed my petite legs over his shoulders, to drive his cock into me even deeper. I closed my eyes, letting my body take over, until I gushed all over his crotch. He pulled his cock out of me and helped me down off the table. I was then swung around by my hair and pushed face down onto the table. His cock entered me again, but this time into my ass, and I let out an even louder moan. He leaned down, his breath was so hot on my skin.

"Shut up bitch, and take it. I know you like this, your pussy's so wet right now," he whispered in my ear.

His fingers explored my insides, as he kept driving his cock in my tight end. I came again drenching his hand, then he shoved his fingers into my mouth so I could taste my sweetness. His cock slid out from between my cheeks and was quickly shoved back into my waiting hole. I held onto the sides of the table with my legs spread at hip width to keep my balance, as he pounded my pussy hard. I heard him let out a moan, and his hot liquid dripped down the insides of my legs. He pulled out his semi-hard cock from my beaten pussy, then zipped up his pants.

"Make sure to put whatever you got into away, and pull the door closed behind you when you leave. Oh, and thanks for the pussy, it was as good as I thought it'd be," he said.

I watched him leave the room before I put my pants back on and tucked my boobs back into my bra, so I could button up my shirt. I never expected the sheriff to be such a good fuck, with a big dick to boot. I finished getting dressed and I made sure that I cleaned up the mess on the floor, with some paper towels I'd found next to the box of rubber gloves. I straightened up the boxes before I left for my room back at the inn...

CHAPTER 23: THE ANSWERS ARE ON THE BOARD

When I returned from the police station, the first thing on my mind was putting the puzzle together. All the pictures and paperwork lay scattered across my bed. Something was still missing. It wasn't just the weapon I still needed. The athame in question could only have belonged to three people, Johnny, Rose, or Magus. I picked up every picture, one, by one, staring blankly at it, then I saw the tattoo on Johnny's wrist. It was still hard to make out, but it looked similar in shape to the one the sheriff had on his wrist. It was several spirals, meeting upward, into what appeared to be, an upside-down L.

I got off the bed and went to the bathroom, when I came back, most of my paperwork was on the floor. I rubbed my arms and walked over to the thermostat, it read seventy-five, but it was more like thirty-five in here. When I turned back toward the bed, the papers and pictures were in a neat pile in the center. On top of the pile was the picture of Johnny and Rose. I picked it up and looked at it, and then I saw something out of the upper right corner of my eye, over by the window. It must have been a flash of light passing by. When I looked back on the bed, the coroner's report with Magus's fingerprints was separated from the other papers. I knew someone was here, but I didn't want to act in such a manner that would scare, or ward off my uninvited guest.

I walked into the closet, where I kept my duffle bag. I pulled out a large white candle, a smudge bundle, and a container of sea salt. After I lit them both, I set them on the floor, in the center of the room, and then I poured the sea salt all around in a circle. I sat down next to the candle and waited. If a spirit were here in the room with me, it would be drawn to the light of the candle, the smell of sage, and the salt would prevent it from attacking me. My breath floated out in a cloud before me. The flame of the candle blew sideways, before it flickered and went out completely.

A silhouette of a woman appeared, for only but a moment, in the far corner of the room, before it vanished. I sat there staring at the corner waiting, afraid if I blinked I'd miss it if it reappeared again. Then the candle in front of me went flying across the room. I could barely catch my breath. My heartbeat slowed down and I went back to the closet to get something else from my bag, that I never leave home without.

I set my board on the table and grabbed my notepad. My pen was placed in the wire of my notebook, so I sat and waited for the planchette to move. I had a strong feeling from the brief glance of the spirit, that it was Rose, but I didn't want to chance it being something else.

"Rose, is that you? It's ok. I'm not here to harm you. I'm here to help you, but I need your help too," I spoke softly.

I waited for the heart-shaped, ivory piece to move across my Ouija board, it had been in my Romani family for generations, and it's never let me down. I heard a rustling and heard the planchette move. It rested on the word 'YES'. Good, this was a start.

"Rose, I need to know who killed you?"

The board that was made out of the heart of a Beech Tree, a wood used a lot by my family, began to shake. I waited with pen in hand, ready to write. The planchette moved two laps around the board, before settling on a J. The board shook again.

"It's all right Rose, I know this has to be new to you, take your time."

The planchette moved to the O. It did another two laps around the board in the opposite direction. It stopped at the H. I waited for it to move again, even though I had an idea of what she was trying to spell. The planchette pointed to me and went backward around the side of the board, with the eye revealing the next letter, N. The ivory plank began to spin, and I'd never seen such a sight, this dead girl was dramatic. It finally stopped spinning in a circle and stopped on the N again, then flew across the board, stopping on the Y.

"Ok, I understand. Johnny caused your death, but I heard that Magus helped. Did Magus assist in your death?"

I could have sworn that I heard the faint sound of crying, and I couldn't possibly understand what Rose must be going through. If life was as difficult as it was with the ability to communicate, it must be hell on the dead, without the ability for communication, whilst being trapped between worlds. The board shook again flipping the planchette upside down. It began to move again, stopping on the letter M. Rose must have gotten the hang of moving the planchette, as it went around the Ouija board with ease. The next letter was A, then G, then U, and rotating around once more, to settle on the S.

"Thank you, Rose. You've helped me a great deal, and I will see to it that I find a way to help you move on," I promised.

The board shook once more, and the planchette circled the board three times, before settling on the letter C. I thought she was finished, I guess not. I wrote down the letter on the paper and waited for the next. The ivory moved again, spelling the next word with ease, O, V, E, and finally stopping on the letter N.

"What do you mean by, 'coven'? Do you mean the coven members that died in the accidents?"

The eye of the planchette showed me the word, 'NO'.

"Is this another coven you speak of?"

'YES', the board revealed.

"Whose coven are you referring to?"

The planchette spelled out, 'JOHNNY' once more.

"Johnny's coven? I thought Johnny's coven members were all dead?"

The planchette showed me the word, 'NO'.

I went over all of it in my head. It didn't make sense to me. If Johnny was dead, and Magus said his coven members had committed suicide, then who was left? Unless Magus, was the other coven member Rose was trying to protect? I had to go see Magus. He would tell me the truth, I just knew it. He had to…

CHAPTER 24: THE COVEN

I went to Magus's house, determined to get some answers. There was something he wasn't telling me, and I was going to find out what it was. He was walking out his front door when I walked up. He greeted me with a smile and a kiss.

"What are you doing here? I was just on my way out," Magus asked.

"I can see that. Where are you headed?"

"Oh, just out for a bit. Would you like to come along? If you need to talk about something, we can talk on the way if you'd like," he offered.

"Sure, I suppose I can. Where are we going?" I questioned.

"Oh, you'll see."

I got into his 64 ½ Mustang, and we drove off to the surprise destination. It was quiet for the first few minutes, until he broke the silence.

"What did you want to talk about?"

"I was curious about how the coven worked out for you, now that all of the members are dead," I inquired.

"Are you asking me, how I celebrate the old ways alone?"

"I guess I am, so to speak."

"A full coven isn't necessary to perform rituals you know. There are solitary practitioners out there. Take for instance the couple, that had been found in the woods dead. Yes, they were part of our coven, but oftentimes they would perform rituals on their own, as a couple. Everyone practices the craft in their own way, whether it's with someone else, or not. Like me now, I was heading into the woods myself to recharge," he added.

"What did you mean by 'our' coven? Was there someone else besides you left?"

"No, I didn't mean to say our, it's a force of habit. Come now, put a smile on those luscious lips of yours, we're almost there."

His warm hand rested on my knee, softly stroking it with his thumb. Chills crept down my spine, settling into my stomach and making me queasy. I wasn't sure why exactly, but I had a strange feeling wash over me, that I couldn't explain…

Magus parked the car at the edge of the woods, on a graveled lot. I looked around when I got out of the car.

"What is this place?" I asked.

"It's a sacred place, come."

He took my hand, as we stepped into the heavily wooded forest. It seemed almost magical, once we stepped inside amongst the trees.

We walked for about a mile before we reached a clearing. A large fire pit graced the center, while a circle of stones enclosed the entire perimeter. A large fallen Oak Tree had been used as a seating area, while several stumps were placed directly across, also for seating.

"This is where the coven gathered, weather permitting of course," Magus sighed.

"It's breathtaking," I said, taking in all of the beauty around me.

Magus turned, pulling me into his kiss. I returned his with eagerness. He pressed me into the tree beside us, holding my hand by the wrists over my head with one hand, while the other squeezed one of my breasts. I became lost in his kiss, and the many questions I had were lost to the moment.

Magus pulled me from the tree and walked me over to the fallen log. He turned me around to face the trees, while he kissed the back of my neck, and his hands explored my body. I was nearly lifted off the ground by my crotch, as he rubbed my cunt through my navy blue dress slacks. I turned my face to him, to receive deep penetrating kisses. His hands unbuckled my thin leather belt and unbuttoned my pants. They immediately fell to my feet, then he pulled my lace black thongs aside, to rub my pussy with freshly moistened fingers. He pushed me over the log, and holding myself up, my ass was in perfect alignment with his loins. I let out a gasp when he entered me slowly, with his hot searing flesh. My legs were shoulder width apart, his hands gripping my hips tight, as he yanked me back onto his cock. His thrusts were powerful, and deep, reaching the farthest depths of my cavity. My wanton cries were lost in the woods, no one could possibly hear me, and then a noise in the distance alerted us both to someone's presence. Magus remained calm and was still balls deep inside me.

"Did you hear that, or was it just me?" I asked.

"I heard it too," he confirmed.

Magus shook his head and regained his former rhythm. He drove his cock in and out of my pussy, teasing me with just its head, his knuckles pressing back, and forth into my ass. I reached one hand around to grab him, pulling his hips to fuck me harder. He started fucking me harder, and then I bent over even further, to receive him even deeper. Blood was rushing to my head, as I tried to keep my balance, while he drove himself harder into my creamy goodness.

Magus stopped all of a sudden.

"I heard something," he said.

"What do you think it was?" I asked.

The sheriff emerged from the canopy.

"What are you doing here, sheriff?" Magus asked.

"I was on the other side of the woods, investigating some noises, that the people up the road said they'd heard," replied the sheriff. "What is she doing here?"

"Magus was initiating me into his coven," I blurted out, unsure what I should have said instead. I was not able to come up with a better excuse, given the circumstances.

"I'll bet he is. I can't believe you're fucking him too. And he's our number one suspect in this case. You city agents have a strange way of outing a suspected murderer," the sheriff commented.

It was really difficult to find the right words, when your pants are down around your ankles, and a dick is in your twat. I was having one of those moments. I tried to reach for my pants, but Magus placed his hands over mine.

Magus withdrew from me, before bending over to help me out of my pants, and then removed my shirt, and bra. He removed the rest of his clothes, and I was speechless, as the sheriff began taking off his clothes too. I got a puss-on just in anticipation alone, for what I thought was about to happen.

"Is he, are we...?"

Magus silenced me, covering his mouth over mine. I was so lost in his kiss, to notice that the sheriff had pulled my hair away from my neck to kiss it. Hands explored my body, mouths took turns with mine, and I couldn't keep my focus on just one of them. I held both men in my hands, a cock for each one, as they took turns fondling my breasts and fingering my pussy. Magus stood before me, kissing my neck, while I stoked his cock, with my right hand. The sheriff was behind me, licking the back of my neck, while I stroked his cock, with my left hand. This was my wildest fantasy come true, as I was sandwiched between both men.

I turned my face to kiss the sheriff, as Magus went down on his knees, to bury his face into my wet muff. He sucked my clit, and then the sheriff reached around to slide two fingers inside. I could hardly contain myself, soaking the sheriff's hand and the priest's face. Magus licked my cum from the sheriff's fingers, before pushing me towards the fallen tree. The sheriff sat down on the log, his large cock standing at attention waiting for me. I straddled the sheriff, who held his cock for me so I could slide down on it. He grabbed my tits, taking turns with each of my hard nipples, as Magus rubbed my clit, while I fucked the sheriff. Then Magus pushed me over, spit on his hand, and then shoved his cock into my ass. I was held tight by both men, as cocks filled every hole. I slowly gyrated my hips up and down each shaft, while taking two different tongues in my mouth. I had two hands to each of my breasts, and then separate mouths suckling each nipple. My moans, echoed throughout the forest, as I took on both men, at once.

Magus pulled his cock from my ass and helped me dismount from the sheriff. I was pulled to Magus who lifted me off the ground. I wrapped my legs around him, as he reached around to my ass, to shove his cock into my pussy. The sheriff walked up behind me, then grabbed my hips, bouncing me up and down on Magus's hard member. The sheriff's cock penetrated my ass, sliding easily inside. Both sets of hands held my ass, pushing me up and down on their cocks skillfully. I kissed Magus fully, searching his mouth with my tongue, as I moved easily between both men, which were now drenched in sweat and with my juices, dripping from my loins. The sounds of their excitement were music to my ears, as they both erupted simultaneously, filling both my holes full of their cum.

I slid down gently between them to the ground, then gathered some napkins I had in my purse. While they didn't suspect I had ulterior motives, besides appearing as though I was simply cleaning myself off, I stuffed the napkins back into my purse. First thing tomorrow morning, I'll take them to the lab.

The sheriff gave me a quick kiss, and without a word walked back into the woods. I finished getting dressed and walked with

Magus back to the car. No words were spoken. What would you say after a night like that? When we arrived back at the inn, Magus just kissed me goodbye, after thanking me for a wild evening, and then drove away. I walked back up to my room and went straight to the bathroom for a shower. I reeked of cock…

CHAPTER 25: PIECING THE PUZZLE TOGETHER

I paced back and forth, in the laboratory hallway, waiting for the results to come back. When the technician came out of his office, I stopped pacing and wiped the sweat from my palms.

"The samples you requested for testing came back positive. I hope that helps you to catch your killer. If you need anything else just give me a call," he informed me.

I sat down on the bench in the hall, while I watched the tech walk away. He was right, I had caught the killer. I had hoped the results of the test had been wrong. My legs dragged, as I tried to carry the weight of my broken heart, back to my empty room.

I couldn't rely on my intuition this time. I had to face the facts now, and the truth of the matter was, that the victim had sexual relations with the one person who had betrayed me. Why would he lie to my face, about not fucking her before she died? Because he was guilty, that's why, and I was too blind by my own lust to see it. Magus fucked Rose, and then killed her in cold blood. I'm sure after that, he couldn't stop himself, and moved on to kill the couple too. Perhaps they knew too much, or they were needed for a blood spell. Either way, I was pissed, and I was going to take his ass down.

I returned to my room, while the thoughts of finally closing this case, tasted bitter in my mouth. Deep down, I still wanted to believe Magus was innocent, that it was only my jealousy, which made me want to lynch him right now. I needed to know the truth. I looked at my notepad, where I had written down what Rose had shown me on the Ouija board. Apparently, I had doodled that symbol, without thinking about it. The tattoo on the sheriff's wrist, and the similar one, that was on Johnny's from the photo. But what was the significance of the symbol? There were still too many questions, which had not been answered, and there was only one way that I was going to get them.

I gathered my Ouija board, candle, and smudge bundle, setting them on the table. I lit the incense and the white pillar candle, then waited for the planchette to move across the wooden board.

"Rose, if you're here, please show yourself. I need your help again."

I rubbed my hands up and down the length of my arms, as my breath slowly floated out before me. The smoke from the sage blew faster across the room, and the flame flickered, before suddenly being snuffed out. She was here.

"Rose, I need to ask you some questions, and I hope you can help me with the answers."

The board scooted to the other side of the table, beside its ivory companion, then the planchette began to move in circles around the board, stopping on the word 'YES'.

"Did you have sexual relations with your priest, before you died?"

The planchette moved to the left, then back to the word 'YES'.

"Did Magus kill you?"

The ivory pointer moved in a complete circle around the board, before settling on the word 'NO'. I thought that was the only answer, until it moved again across the board settling on a

'J', then on an 'O', and then continued spelling out the remaining letters, 'H', 'N', 'N', 'Y'. I had my answer, but how did he manage to kill her, if he had possessed her? It was as if I was getting nowhere fast, and my patience was wearing thin. I stood up to pace the room, and then nearly shit myself when the board was flipped onto the floor.

I stopped, and fell to the floor, as Rose appeared before me. She extended her hand to me, and I responded as if on impulse, extending my hand to her as well. Tiny sparks of an electrical charge shot from my fingers, as if I'd touched a metal object or after stroking a cat. The sparks grew brighter, until I had to look away. When I turned to look again, I could no longer see her image. I quickly ran to the bathroom flinging up the lid of the toilet to vomit. After I expelled the contents of my stomach, I clenched it, falling to the floor in the fetal position. The tile was cold, but not as cold as my insides felt…

I felt monstrous possessing the agent, but it was the only way I could help her. After all, she had gone this far in trying to help me; the least I could do was return the favor. I wasn't certain what the best approach was, to let her know that I was here inside her, but I had to just come out with it.

"Anna?" *I whispered.*

I sat up from the bathroom floor, sure as I was sitting here, freezing my ass off that someone had said my name.

"*Anna,*" Rose said again.

What the fuck? There it was again.

"Hello, is someone here?" I said, stepping out into the room.

"*Yes, you can hear me?*"

I sat down on the bed.

"I can hear you. Who are you, and why does it sound like you're in my fucking head?"

"*It's me, Rose. I am in your head, actually. There is really no delicate way to put this. I possessed you. I'm terribly sorry for that, but it was the only way I could truly help you."*

I had no words. Then I found some.

"Why? Why me?"

"Because you're the only one who can help me. But we must go to Magus immediately, I'll explain on the way," Rose stated.

"Is there something I should know, about how all of this works first? Am I going to start flying through the air, spewing pee soup, and fucking myself with a crucifix, or something?"

I couldn't help but laugh, since I'd almost done that myself, all but the spewing of the pea soup, and masturbating with a cross.

"No, nothing of the sort. I promise I will not harm you. But we must go now, we don't have much time," Rose stated.

I walked out of my room heading in the direction of Magus's house on foot, while Rose explained everything to me that had happened the night of her death...

CHAPTER 26: THE CONFRONTATION

When we arrived at the street directly across from Magus's house, Rose had me stop for a minute.

"Anna, I'm going to have to take over now. You can still see and feel everything, but I'll be in control of your body."

"Why? Is that really necessary?" I asked the dead girl, in my head.

"It's just in case it's not Magus. If I take over, then I will be able to tell whether or not Johnny has possessed him," Rose explained.

"He didn't seem possessed to me?"

"Do you feel possessed?"

"Well, no, not really," I admitted.

"That's my point. Johnny will be extremely cautious when interacting with others, especially those closest to Magus."

I was so afraid to think right now, for fear that Rose would be able to hear my thoughts. I really didn't want a catfight over a man in my head right now.

"If you're wondering whether or not I know about you and Magus, don't worry, I'm not upset. I'm actually happy for him. What happened between Magus and me on the night of my death, was something that just happened," she informed.

"And if you hadn't died that night?"

"I would probably still be with him. I did love him, but it was on a

deeper level. It was spiritual," Rose added.

"I'm so sorry all of this happened to you, Rose," I said tenderly.

"It's not your fault. But I couldn't live with myself if this were to happen to anyone else. This ends here, and now."

It was the strangest feeling moving, but not by my own will, as Rose walked on to Magus's house.

Rose knocked on the door, and we waited patiently for Magus to open it. He opened the door and smiled.

"Hello, Rose. So good to see you again."

"I'm sorry that, I can't say the same to you."

"Why are you just standing there? Run damn you!" Rose shouted in my head.

"I can't," I whispered.

"What do you mean, you can't?"

Johnny grabbed my arms and dragged us into the house. The furniture had been cleared from the living room, all but a chair, and the altar. He pushed me down in the chair, binding my wrists and ankles to the chair legs.

"I knew sooner or later you would find me, Rose. It was just a matter of time before our spirits began to pull one another back together. And now that I have you, I won't let you go ever again," Johnny said, from his vessel, Magus.

"Johnny, please don't do this," Rose begged.

He walked over to me raised my chin and kissed me. I would have spat at him if I could move.

"Why can't I move you?" Rose asked.

"I was wondering when you were going to ask that? See, dear Magus is the last generation, of a long line of necromancers. By being in control of his body, I can also use his powers, even if he's never used them himself. I don't even think he knew he could actually. But that's his loss and my gain. Any more questions, before I begin the spell?"

"What will happen to Magus, and Anna when your spell is complete?"

"Oh, wouldn't you like to know? I wouldn't worry about them right now. Just relax, it will all be over soon enough."

"Johnny, please let them go, they're innocent. It's me that you want. I'll be with you forever, without a fight, if you promise that you'll release them."

The smack echoed throughout the room. Tears came to my eyes from the sting upon my cheek.

"I don't trust you, Rose. I'm sorry I struck you, but it has to be this way."

He walked over to the altar, to prepare for the spell.

"Everything has been made ready, our spirits will be united this night, and be merged together forever throughout the centuries," Johnny declared.

"It looks like you won't get that chance, my love. The sheriff is here and will arrest Magus for sure, now that he's caught in the act with his next victim. Did you really think the murders you committed with his body would go unnoticed? There were fingerprints left everywhere from your sloppiness. I'm sure if you turn his body in to the authorities now, he won't get the death penalty, he could even plead insanity. Let Magus go, and I will leave Anna to join you in the afterlife, you have my word," Rose promised.

Johnny said nothing, as the front door opened. The sheriff came in, and Johnny immediately put his hands in the air.

"Oh, officer, please don't arrest me for all those murders, I've committed. It wasn't me, I swear."

The sheriff's cold gaze fell upon me as he laughed. He handed Johnny a bag that he'd brought in with him. Johnny took it to the altar, then began to remove all the remaining ingredients needed for the spell.

"What are you going to do with her?" the sheriff asked, as he walked over to me. "Do we get to include some sex magic in this spell?"

He licked the side of my face and ran his hand up my thigh. Johnny quickly snatched him up by his throat.

"Right now, that's my bitch you're licking. I suggest next time, to keep that tongue inside your fucking head, or I'll cut it the fuck out. Understand?"

The sheriff nodded.

"Good. When I'm finished she will be all mine," Johnny stated.

"What about the detective? Can't I have her when you're finished merging your spirits?"

"No, because she will no longer be the detective."

"I thought you were going to just merge your spirits?" The sheriff inquired.

"I had a change of plans. After spending so much time in Magus's body, I had forgotten what it felt like to be a man again, a whole man," Johnny admitted.

"So, what are you saying? You're going to kill him, and take over his body?"

"No! How can you do this! Johnny, please don't kill them," Rose cried out.

Johnny turned to me and pressed his fingers together.

"Shh. No more from you," he hissed.

I couldn't speak.

"I'm not killing anyone, if you both must know. I'm simply going to expel their spirits, from out of their own bodies. They will move on into the otherworld, unharmed," Johnny promised.

"That's going to take some serious magic, master," the sheriff said.

"No more than an exorcism. It's actually easier to expel them, and then you'll hand fast us, so our spirits can be together forever, even after these bodies die. I'll find us new bodies to possess and do the same thing, it's simple really," Johnny explained.

"Am I ready for level one now?"

"You will be, after assisting in this ritual."

"I'll go change into my robes then," the sheriff said.

My Love Inside Me

I watched helplessly from inside my body. I could see and hear everything, but I couldn't respond or control my body. Rose wasn't doing much better, while under Johnny's control, and right now, we were both fucked…

CHAPTER 27: THE MERGING OF THE SOULS

The thought finally occurred to me, that I could still communicate with Rose. If she could hear my thoughts, then she would be able to hear me speak to her.

"Rose, can you hear me?" I asked.

"Yes, can you hear my thoughts, because my mouth has been made to keep quiet? I'm so sorry my dead, asshole, ex-boyfriend, is going to try and expel yours, and Magus's spirits," Rose replied.

"I can't really say that I've been in worse situations than this, but I have a plan," I said.

"What's that?" Rose inquired.

"Do you know any counter spells to control Johnny's spirit, which would allow Magus to regain control over his body?" I asked.

"Only the one that Magus used on him when he had possessed me. But I have to say it out loud, and right now I'm bound, literally," Rose stated.

"He'll have to let you speak sometime. Could you force out some tears? Maybe that would be enough to get his attention, at least to allow you to speak. Would that give you enough time to say the spell?" I questioned.

"Let's hope so," she replied.

The sheriff returned dressed in his robes, then assisted Johnny with the preparations for the spell. I forced tears to my eyes, and waited for Johnny to notice.

"What is the matter? You should be happy. It's almost time to begin the ceremony, and then we'll be together forever. You want us to be together forever don't you?" Johnny asked.

When I didn't say anything, he waved his hand over my face.

"I do apologize, I'd almost forgotten that I held your tongue for you. Now, tell me that you're happy," he ordered.

"I am happy. I know now that we are meant to be, and that I want to be with you also, forever," Rose lied.

"Now, wait for the right moment. After the chant is complete let me take over," I said.

Rose began to chant the spell in Latin, and Johnny fell to his knees.

"Stop herbefore she finishes the spell!" Johnny shouted.

Rose kept chanting, and right as the last word was spoken, I regained control of my body. I twisted my wrists, allowing me to slip through the knot. When the sheriff tried to grab me, I brought my head forward. He fell to the floor immediately. I quickly leaned over to untie my ankles, then got up from the chair.

The sheriff came at me again, then I grabbed one of the vases off the mantle, and shattered it, as it bounced off the back of his head. He went down for a brief moment, and then Johnny got up and came after me. The spell didn't hold.

"What's the spell?" I asked.

"Watch out, Anna!" Rose shouted from my head.

Johnny and the sheriff tackled me onto the floor. I had no other choice, and bit the sheriff's ear clean off. He cradled his head and blood spilled out onto the floor, while he lay screaming in the fetal position.

Johnny grabbed me from behind, dragging me by my hair

to the altar. He held me down, slicing my wrist over the chalice. He began to chant in Latin, the merging of the souls spell.

"Now would be a good time to take over, and recite your spell again," I said.

Rose took over and began to try the spell again. Johnny never slowed down, so she began to chant even louder. He finally stopped chanting, and Rose continued to chant in Latin. The Priest turned to me with his own eyes.

"Rose, is that you?" Magus asked softly.

"Magus!" Rose exclaimed.

We embraced. It felt good to be in his arms again.

"It's me for now, but there's not a lot of time. We must act fast."

Suddenly the sheriff cocked the trigger of his gun. Rose let me take over, and I went after the sheriff. We fell to the floor, the gun went off and the bullet hit the empty chair. We wrestled on the floor for a few minutes, and then I punched him on the side of his missing ear. He screamed in pain, releasing his grip on the gun, and allowing me to grab it. I quickly stood up, then he grabbed my ankle, pulling me to the floor. He was trying to pull himself between my legs, when I shot him between his eyes. I pushed his body off of me, and tossed the gun aside.

Magus helped me up and embraced me.

"Come, we must hurry, I need you to help me with the spell, Rose," the priest said.

I let Rose take over once again, as she and Magus knelt before the altar.

"This is our only chance, to be rid of him for good. Are you ready?" Magus said.

"More than you'll ever know. Let's send that sorry bastard to the afterlife," Rose said smiling.

CHAPTER 28: THE BANISHMENT

Magus and Rose held hands, and began the chant to expel Johnny from the priest's body. The lights in the house began to flicker. Then he began to twitch and shake.

"Magus, are you all right?" Rose asked.

He shook his head.

"We must keep chanting," he said trembling.

I held his hand tightly, trying to not break the bond. I tried to use all my energy to free Johnny from Magus's body. The room went completely dark, and then he fell to his knees. I never let go of his hand. I wasn't giving up.

A bright light emerged from Magus's body, hovering over him. As the light began to fade, a silhouette of a man began to form. It was Johnny. He was now standing next to Magus's limp body.

"It's not over, Rose. No matter if you banish me, I will return and find you, that I swear," Johnny declared.

Electricity sparked from the side of my face, as Johnny touched me. I couldn't help the tears, which rolled off my cheeks, but I knew I had to say goodbye.

"I did love you once, but I will not let anyone else die for your selfish desires. Goodbye, Johnny," Rose said.

Magus sat up and saw Johnny standing alongside him.

"Hurry, it must be now, before he has a chance to take over again!" Magus shouted.

We began to chant again in Latin, this time it was a spell to banish his soul into the afterlife forever. Objects flew around the room, and the glass in the lights grew hot until they shattered. Johnny wasn't going to go down easily. We chanted even louder, and watched as Johnny returned to the bright ball of light. It began going in crazy circles over our heads, picking up speed, until it seemed to explode. Several tiny bursts from the giant ball of light separated, and then one by one, the tiny lights faded until they all vanished.

Magus smiled, pulling Rose into his arms.

"He's at rest now, may he go in peace," the priest said.

"Oh, Magus I can't believe it's finally over," Rose said crying.

"Yes, my dear it is, and you are now free of him forever," he added.

I sat up and looked my priest lovingly into his hazel eyes. The look on his face told me, that he knew what I was about to say.

"Now, it's time for me to go. I'm not meant to stay here. When you helped take my life, I knew that it wasn't my time to go then, but I had no other choice. And I'm sorry to have dragged you into all this. Please forgive me?" Rose asked.

"There's nothing to forgive my child," he said before kissing me tenderly.

"You have to be the one to do it," I said, wiping the tears from his face.

"I don't want to let you go," Magus said.

"You have to. It's not fair to Anna for me to stay in her body, not after all she has done to help save us," Rose added.

"I love you, and I always will."

"I know. I have always loved you, too."

I kissed him passionately one last time, before I began to say my goodbyes.

"Anna, I want to thank you so much for helping me, and for saving Magus. If it weren't for you, I would have been connected to Johnny for all of eternity, and who knows if he would've stopped killing, even after he got what he wanted. Thank you," Rose said.

"That's just part of the job description. Not to rush anyone, but could I have my body back now?" I asked.

"Yes, of course. Magus, it's time," Rose told him.

Magus let out a sigh and held Anna's hand, reciting the same spell that was used to expel Johnny. Only this time, I would be released to move on into the light, and not explode. When I was finally free, I looked down at Magus and Anna.

Rose stood in her caporal form before Magus and I. She touched the side of his face, smiling at him one last time before she spoke.

"I will always be grateful to the both of you. Thank you. And Magus, I will always love you," her voice echoed, those last words, as a bright light enveloped her.

We turned our heads away from the blinding light. Once the light began to fade, we turned to watch, as it slowly went away. Her spirit was finally free to move on…

CHAPTER 29: CASE CLOSED

I called the deputy and told him, that I had apprehended the killer. When he arrived with extra manpower, he found they weren't needed, the suspect was already dead. I told him everything that had happened. The sheriff had been using Magus's prints to cover his own tracks, so he could pin the murders on him. When I came to arrest Magus, the sheriff had him tied to a chair, to use him one last time to kill me, but I stopped him before he had a chance. I told the deputy that I shot the sheriff, in self-defense. The murderer had been stopped, case closed…

Magus took me back to my hotel, so I could gather my things. We hadn't spoken a word since we left the house after he'd given his statement to the deputy, who would later be sworn in by the mayor, as the new sheriff. Once we entered my room, it was on.

Our mouths locked instinctively, and then we began to remove each other's clothes, without any words between us. Only the soft cries escaping our mouths, as we began to pleasure one another with eager tongues, were heard. I traced his body with my fingers, to ingrain every curve of his muscles into memory. He trembled when my hands slid along his sides, as I went down on my knees to take his swollen cock into my hungry mouth. His fingers combed through my hair, and his head lay back with closed eyes. I massaged his balls with one hand, while I held his cock with the other, as my head bobbed up and down on him. I licked down his shaft to his nut sack, gently sucking each one, the saltiness of his balls went unnoticed, as I was only aware of the pleasure I was giving. He moaned deeply and pulled me by my hair to kiss me again. We slowly walked from the door to the bed. He pushed me back, taking my legs and setting them over his shoulders. I threw my head back into the soft mattress, as he thrust his tongue deep into my pussy. I thrashed about, grabbing the long brown hair and trying to pull his face closer to my crotch, as he sucked and nibbled the hard pink knob under my hood. Two fingers pushed knuckles deep into me, rubbing the upper wall of my cavity. I came instantly, as he pressed into my G-spot. He sucked my creamy center, until I glazed his entire face.

When he came up for air, he wiped me off his bearded face. He hovered over me, leaning down so I could share my flavor. We kissed for what seemed to be for hours, and I could no longer stand for this torturous lovemaking, I was ready to be fucked. I reached between my legs to grab the hard member taunting me, by rubbing against my thighs. I pulled him towards me, rubbing his head between my wet folds. He pulled away at first, teasing me, and then he took himself in his hand guiding his cock into my eager cunt.

I arched my hips up, so he could penetrate me fully. He pounded my pussy hard, thrusting his cock deep into my wet hole. I closed my eyes and let out a deep moan. His kisses were hot on my neck, as he continued to make a trail until he found a hard nipple to latch on to. I pressed my body closer to his, wrapping my arms around his shoulders, and my legs around his waist. We moved as one, with the rhythm of our beating hearts, finding each other's mouths once again.

My pussy began to contract from the pulsating cock buried within me, moving within me until I came all over him. My body became limp with pleasure, as he flipped me over onto my knees. He pushed his cock balls deep in me once again, continuing his assault within my creamy center.

Magus pulled me up on my knees, turning my chin to accept his kiss. He grabbed hold of my bouncing breasts, while he bounced me up and down on his shaft. Then he let go of one of my tits, to rub my swollen clit with his fingers. Cum dripped from his balls, onto the white bed sheets, as he got me off again. Then he pushed me back down on all fours, holding my hips to drive him home. Hot liquid rushed inside me. He leaned over my back with heavy breath, beating down on my wet skin. We both fell to our sides, as we were finally spent. I curled up into his nook, as we lay there without a word between us. The loud beating in our chests seemed to take over the silence, as our heavy breathing had begun to settle down.

I looked up at him, his eyes were closed. When I made a move to get up, he grabbed my hand.

"Going somewhere?"

"I'm sorry, but I have to go."

"You're not leaving town yet, are you?"

"I'm afraid so."

"But I finally had the chance to be with you, with it being me for a change. Why the rush?"

"Because there are other people who need me out there, and more cases to solve. It's nothing personal, just the way it is. I don't have room in my life for love, I just fuck, and run."

"I feel so used," Magus said smiling.

"Should I leave money on the nightstand?" I asked.

"You're so witty."

While I was putting my clothes back on, Magus picked up my notepad from the floor.

"Is this yours?"

"Oh, yes. I must have knocked it off the table."

He handed it to me, but before I placed it inside my bag, I decided to see if he knew what the symbol was.

"I was wondering if you knew what this symbol was, or if it

meant anything?"

Magus took the notepad and looked at the symbol. He passed it back to me without a word.

"Well, what is it?"

"It's the Celtic symbol for power. At least one of them, there are several varying symbols out there. But this is the one Johnny used, for his coven. Why do you ask?" Magus questioned.

"Oh, no reason. I noticed the sheriff had one on his wrist too, but I never put the two of them together, until the sheriff tried to kill me. So the symbol holds no other meaning besides power?" I asked.

"No, not really. Why don't you come back to bed? Stay a little while longer. You're the best piece of ass, I've had in a long time," he said smiling.

I finished shoving the rest of my shit in my duffle bag, and then looked up at Magus and smiled.

"I try. Now, are you going to help me carry down my bags, or do I have to do it all by my lonesome?"

"Sure, it's the least I could do after a lay like that," he teased.

We walked out to the parking lot and set the bags down on the concrete.

"Could you lend me a hand with the tarp?" I asked.

Magus grabbed the front left corner of the grey canvas, helping me roll it up over the car. His gaze immediately fell to the chrome fenders, as the rest of the tarp was removed, his eyes grew even bigger at the sight before him. I finished rolling up the tarp and laughed at Magus's gaping mouth.

"Is this, your car?"

"Yes, it is," I said proudly.

"Is this what I think it is? How did you come by this, I thought they were a ghost?"

"It is a ghost, but I just got lucky I suppose," I stated.

Magus gently ran his hands along the side of the 1959 Dodge, Silver Challenger. He caressed every curve, as if it were a woman he was trying to please.

"I can't believe she's yours. I'm so jealous right now," he said.

"Don't hate me, because I have a cool car," I teased.

I walked around the car, after stuffing the tarp in the trunk, and then kissed Magus one last time. When I opened the car door to get in, Magus gave me a strange glance.

"You're not really an FBI Agent, are you?"

"No, I'm not," I replied.

"Then, what are you?"

"Let's just say I'm kind of like a bounty hunter, but for unruly spirits," I said, then slid down onto the bench seat, and shut the door.

"Where are you headed now?"

"I'm going wherever the spirits lead me," I said.

I turned the key, and the rumble of the Flathead Getaway 6 engine vibrated my seat. I rolled down the window to wave, as I slowly drove out of the parking lot and was ready to hit the open road.

Magus watched as I drove off, and then turned back around, smiling wickedly…

"That was the story of how my life ended, but it wasn't in vain. The sacrifices I had made, saved lives. Even though my own sacrifice was the biggest one of them all."

About the Author

Rose Marie Machario is an author, actress, model, filmmaker, and producer at Machario Productions, to include films Give My Love To Rose, An Affair To Remember, and An Affair To Forget.

Rose has worked in several principal roles, and has been featured in various television shows such as Ozark, The Originals, Nashville, Homicide Hunter, Killer Couples, Murder Chose Me, Murder Comes to Town, Snapped, #Murder, Justice by Any Means, Notorious, Fatal Attraction, Murder Mystery, Murder Decoded, American Nightmare, and Mark of a Killer. Her movie credits include Tag, Super Fly, The Road Less Traveled, The Last Movie Star, and Best Clowns.

Then from onscreen to print, Rose can be seen on the cover of a few online magazines such as February 2016 issue of Hell on Heelz Magazine, and March 2017 issue of Electric Pinup Magazine, and also featured in several other national and international online magazines as an alternative, pinup, and tattooed model.

Rose is also a published author of the high fantasy series, Majick Of The Chosen Ones, featuring three books from that series, The Amulet Of Elements, The Fate Of The Realm, and The Path Of Destiny. She recently debutes as a supernatural horror writer, with My Love Inside Me, and has written a few screenplays, and a column called Always Dream Big.

In her spare time she is an Inspirational (Tarot) Reader, enjoys a daily routine of yoga, loves to cook, and cuddling up with her fur-babies while binge watching her favorite television shows, and movies.

45656337R00107